CONFESSIONS

CONFESSIONS

A NOVEL BY

KATE BRIAN

SIMON PULSE

New York London Toronto Sydney

SIMON PULSE
An imprint of Simon & Schuster Children's Publishing Division
1230 Avenue of the Americas, New York, NY 10020

Produced by Alloy Entertainment
151 West 26th Street, New York, NY 10001

Cover design by Julian Peploe
Book design by Amy Trombat
Typography by Andrea C. Uva
The text of this book was set in Filosofia.

Manufactured in the United States of America
First Simon Pulse edition April 2007

6 8 10 9 7

Library of Congress Control Number 2007922046

ISBN-13: 978-1-4169-1876-9
ISBN-10: 1-4169-1876-0

VULTURES

When faced with tragedy, we gather as many people around us as we possibly can. Mere acquaintances become best friends. Enemies become kindred spirits. We need people so later we can look back and say, "I went through that with them." People who can remind us that what we experienced, what we felt, was real. That we were there. So on that morning in early December, when we were all roused from our cozy dorm rooms just as the gray mist of dawn had started to rise, everyone set about finding that group to cling to. Someone to link arms with to make us feel less vulnerable, less unsure. Less like the world was on the verge of caving in.

My group had found me. They had huddled around me from the moment we stepped out of Billings House and hadn't broken ranks once on the slow walk across the Easton Academy campus to the chapel. Noelle. Ariana. Kiran. Natasha. Then, further out, Cheyenne, Rose, London, Vienna, and the others, their shoes crunching through the frost-caked grass. They wanted me to feel safe. To feel protected.

Or so it must have looked to the outside world. In my world—in my head—I was no longer sure of anything.

Where had the police taken Josh? Was he scared? Was he cold? What was he thinking? I kept seeing his face. The look of shock as they dragged him away. The pleading in his eyes. I kept hearing him tell me he could never hurt Thomas. Could I believe him? Could I believe anyone at Easton anymore?

It's all lies, Reed, Taylor had written to me. *All of it.*

There was a shout in the distance. Someone near me flinched. Everyone paused and turned, but there was nothing to see. Two crows cawed their way across the gray sky overhead, and for a long moment no one moved. Hundreds of steaming clouds of breath mingled in the air around us. Silence.

"Let's go," Noelle said finally, nudging us forward.

I looked at her face for the first time all morning. The cold had turned her cheeks pink, and her brown eyes were bright. Beautiful as ever. She smiled at me reassuringly as the wind tossed her thick brown hair across her face. I didn't smile back.

Footsteps jogged to catch up with us. Soon Dash McCafferty and Gage Coolidge were upon us, falling into step.

"Hey." Dash kissed Noelle's temple. His blond hair had been blown up on the side by the wind and stuck there, making him look even more like an Abercrombie model than usual.

"What was that?" Noelle asked, glancing back over her shoulder.

"Vultures," Gage said through his teeth. His striped rugby scarf was tossed around his neck and chin, and his hair was slick with water from the shower. He must have been freezing, but he was too cool to show it.

"Reporters," Dash amended. "They're camped out down by the gates. Dean Marcus had them locked last night after the police left. My father got a phone call an hour ago informing him of heightened security measures. They must've called all the parents."

"Fab," Kiran said. "Bet my mother *loved* that wake-up call."

"One of 'em scaled the fence, though. Trey was on his run and saw Scat 'escorting' some slag with a video camera off campus," Gage informed us. He made a fist with one leather-gloved hand and pressed it into his other palm. "Fucking vultures."

"Scat's the head of security," Natasha, my roommate, informed me, noting the question in my eyes.

I had seen him before. Large man. No neck. Perpetual scowl. I never realized anyone knew his name.

"So we're locked in," Kiran stated. She shivered and lifted the fur collar of her coat higher on her throat so that it grazed her perfect cheekbones. With her huge sunglasses covering her eyes and her dark hair down around her face, she looked for all the world like a starlet trying to avoid the paparazzi.

"For now," Dash told us. "Until they figure out what to do next."

"What's to figure?" Noelle asked. "They have the murderer in custody now, don't they?"

I wasn't sure whose scathing look was more deadly, mine or Dash's. Probably his, since I was fairly certain he'd never looked at Noelle like that before in all the time they'd known one another, which was forever. We had arrived at the open chapel entry. The door was flanked by the Ketlar advisor, Mr. Cross, and my history teacher, Mr. Barber. Dash turned, jaw clenched, and stormed inside without another word to his beloved girlfriend.

"What's his malfunction?" Noelle said.

"I think there's a little something called innocent until proven guilty?" Natasha replied. Noelle rolled her eyes. Rolled her eyes at the suggestion that perhaps Josh Hollis, our friend, had perhaps *not* cold-bloodedly murdered Thomas Pearson.

"Let's keep it moving, ladies," Mr. Barber said, waving his hand. He stared past us with piercing eyes, as if keeping the lookout for some unknown danger. "Let's keep it moving."

I stepped into the hushed chapel and started down the aisle to the sophomore section. A chill rushed through me at the sudden loss of the Billings Girls' surrounding body heat, but I felt somehow free. I realized fully for the first time that I'd been aching to get away from them. To be alone and have some time to think. Then a cold hand closed around my wrist.

"We'll be right back here if you need us, Reed," Ariana said, her ice blue eyes boring straight through me.

I tried to pull my arm away, but she held firm.

"I know," I told her, speaking my first words of the day.

She released me and smiled angelically. "Good."

It's all lies, Reed, Taylor had written. *All of it.*

I turned my back to her and found my seat.

NEW RULES

I left my coat on and buttoned, the better to make a fast escape when it was all over. The murmuring in the chapel had a panicked quality. It was obvious that the seniors and juniors near the back knew exactly what had happened, while most of the sophomores and all of the freshmen were speculating cluelessly. The difference was in their eyes. The older students' eyes were narrowed—stunned but pensive. The younger kids had a wide-eyed, what-the-hell-is-going-on look about them. These were the details I noted as I sat. Paying attention to them kept my mind off things I didn't want to think about.

"Do you have any idea what's going on?" Constance Talbot asked, sliding into the seat next to mine. Her red hair was back in a sloppy French braid, good for hiding the fact that it hadn't been washed. Colorful shafts of light came through the stained glass windows and bathed her face in pink and yellow. She shimmied out of her gray wool coat and bent forward, trying to catch my eye. "Reed? Come on. I know you know."

She assumed this because I was in Billings. And the Billings Girls knew everything. Which maybe I did, but too late. Always too late.

"Reed?" she sounded more urgent, concerned. "Reed? Are you okay?"

The chapel doors closed. Silence fell. Everyone faced forward. Even Constance. It was easy to quiet this place when the students were salivating for news. My gloved hands closed into fists on my lap. Dean Marcus stepped up to the altar at the front of the chapel. His wrinkled face looked pale and tired. He pressed both hands into the surface of the podium.

"Students, can I have your attention, please?" he said, even though he already had it. His voice was deep and authoritative. It didn't match his wan appearance. "Thanks to all of you for gathering here quickly and in an orderly fashion. As always I'm impressed with the level of maturity of our student body. I only ask that when you hear what I have to say, you maintain your calm. Right now, more than ever, this community needs to know that it can rely on itself and its members, that we will not let one another down. These are the high standards I expect from the students of Easton. These are the high standards you should expect from yourselves."

There was a lot of shifting and a few murmurs. Out of the corner of my eye, I saw Constance look at me.

Dean Marcus took a deep breath. "Students, I regret to inform you that a member of the junior class, Joshua Hollis, has been arrested on suspicion of murder."

"What?"

"Oh my God."

"You've gotta be kidding me. Josh Hollis is a Boy Scout!" someone shouted.

"It's always the quiet ones," someone else said solemnly.

There was no stopping the din now. It consumed the chapel. Constance grabbed my hand. All she got was a cold fist.

"Students! Students!" the dean shouted.

He was ignored. Everyone was busy gasping, blabbering about how they couldn't believe it. Someone, somewhere, was crying. Crying. Who the hell was crying?

"I can't believe this. I can't believe someone we know *killed* someone. . . ."

He didn't. He didn't do it. Stop saying he did it.

"Reed. Oh my God. Did you know about this? Are you okay?" Constance asked me, turning so that our knees were touching. "Reed, you're freaking me out here. Say something."

I wanted to. I didn't want to freak her out. But I knew that if I opened my mouth or so much as truly looked at her, I would break down. And I couldn't have that. Not now. Not yet.

"Silence!" Dean Marcus roared. He brought his fist down several times on the surface of the podium. "I will have silence!"

That did it. The place was suddenly as still as night. His watery eyes traveled the room slowly.

"I realize that this is difficult news to hear, and that it is even harder to accept, and that is why I wanted you to hear it from me.

I wanted to tell you this before it came out in the newspapers, before rumors started flying, because I wanted to remind you that we here at Easton support one another. Let us all remember one of the most important laws of our society—that a person is innocent until he or she is proven guilty," the dean said, leaning over the podium. Somewhere, I knew Natasha was smirking. "If Mr. Hollis is proven to be guilty, we will deal with it then, but until that time he is still a member of this community, and as such he is due our respect and support."

For that one moment, I liked the dean. I liked him very much.

"Now, I don't have to tell you that the next few weeks are going to be a trying time for this academy," the dean continued. "Not only do you all face the challenge of final exams, but there will be reporters, gossip hounds, and so-called newspeople, all bent on bringing this institution to its knees. We all know how cruel the media can be, and they adore a scandal like this one. I also know how seductive the spotlight can be, so I have taken steps to ensure that none of you are tempted. From today on, the gates around this campus are closed to outsiders. No one other than your immediate family—your parents, your guardians—will be allowed on campus."

There was a long pause. No one moved.

"More important, no students will be allowed to leave this campus unless in the company of a parent or guardian."

This got a reaction. How could it not? I had been hearing murmurs for weeks about trips to New York and Boston. Shopping excursions, club-hopping, posh holiday dinners at exclusive restaurants. In one fell swoop the dean was robbing these privileged kids of their lifestyles.

"Do not even think about testing me on this one, people. It is nonnegotiable," the dean continued. "If you do attempt to test me, there will be dire consequences."

Once again his glare set upon each of us. The faculty members who stood along the walls seemed to crowd in toward us, like they were ready to grab anyone who tried to make a break for it.

"We will concentrate on our studies. We will remember what this institution is all about, and we will live it every day. Tradition. Honor. Excellence."

"Tradition. Honor. Excellence," the student body mumbled grumpily.

Like it was all about them. Like the most important thing said at this assembly had been about the locked gates, the new restrictions.

Like Josh had already been forgotten.

MOTIVE

For once I didn't even bother getting food. Not that I'd been able to eat much lately, but usually I at least went through the motions, got myself a trayful of whatever and maybe tried to take at least one bite. But I was tired of pretending. Who the hell was I keeping up appearances for, anyway? I walked along the wall of the cavernous cafeteria, past all the quaint paintings of rural New England set in their ornate frames, listening to the chatter bouncing off the domed ceiling. The students around me stared and whispered, but I was used to that by now.

I sat at our usual table, alone, and slumped in my chair with one question plaguing my mind: Who *had* killed Thomas? I knew Josh hadn't done it. Knew it in my bones. But if he hadn't, then who had? I had to know. More important, the police had to know. If the real killer was exposed, they would have to let Josh go. As simple as that. But who else could possibly have done it? Who had a reason to kill Thomas?

Noelle and the others arrived with their trays of hot oatmeal, toasted bagels, and steaming coffee, and crowded in around me.

"Reed, I know you're depressed and all, but bad posture isn't going to make it any better," Kiran said. She perched on the edge of her own chair, slim legs crossed at the ankle, and lifted a heavy, scented magazine from her bag.

"Give her one day to wallow, Emily Post," Noelle said.

Kiran shrugged. "Fine, but when you're a hunchback at forty, don't come crying to me."

Dash dropped like a boulder into the chair across from Noelle and stabbed repeatedly at his oatmeal with his spoon.

"Problem?" Noelle asked, arching a brow.

Dash stared. "No. Everything's fine, actually. One friend dead, one in jail. I don't know about you guys, but I'm feeling pretty damn upbeat."

"I just can't believe he did it," Noelle pondered. "Little Josh Hollis, a murderer."

"You're the one who decided it was him," I blurted.

All movement at the table stopped. Like someone had hit the pause button on my life.

"Excuse me?" Noelle said.

I could rewind. Take it back. But I didn't want to. The incredulity with which she'd said those two words made me want to hurl something at her. Last night she had been all cocky assurances that Josh was a psycho. That he had potentially murdered before. She had no right to act surprised and appalled.

"You! You're the one who called the police on him," I said. "And now all of a sudden you're shocked?"

Noelle slowly placed her glass of juice down on the table. "Let me clarify something, Reed. I was suspicious before, not certain."

"Well, I don't know what makes you so certain now," Dash said. "Just because the police arrested him, that doesn't make him guilty."

"Boy has a point," Natasha said.

"Thank you. I'm sorry, but I have a hard time believing that one of us could kill someone," Dash said, the color in his face rising.

"It happens all the time," Ariana said lightly, as though she were announcing the weather forecast. "People snap."

"Yeah, but not Josh. The guy's like a Disney character," Dash said.

"All I know is, I'm glad it's over," Kiran said, flipping blithely through her magazine. "I've been so stressed out, I missed all the calls for the good spring shows. If that slut Melenka gets first curtain at Stella McCartney, *I'm* going to kill someone."

My fingers closed around Natasha's butter knife. Natasha's hand gently covered mine.

"Wow, Kiran, you just rose to previously uncharted levels of shallowness," Natasha said.

"Do you come with a mute button?" Kiran responded. "Because I, for one, am sick of your high-and-mightiness."

"Well, well! The bitch is back!" Gage said, patting Kiran on the back so hard she flinched. "It's a pleasure."

He was right. Kiran was in rare form. Possibly even meaner than she'd been before Thomas's disappearance. These people really thought it was over. Josh had done it. Throw away the key.

"It just doesn't make any sense, that's all I'm saying," Gage put in. "Don't you need a motive for murder? What the hell would Josh's motive have been? He and Thomas were so close they were practically gay."

A couple of people chuckled. My stomach clenched.

"Wow. So I guess we *all* took our immaturity pills this morning," Natasha said pointedly. She'd just been outed to all of us a couple of months back, which made Gage's joke particularly appalling.

"No offense," Gage said, without an ounce of sincerity. "All I'm saying is, maybe it was a crime of passion," he suggested, looking directly at me.

Ariana coughed and quickly covered her mouth with her napkin. Noelle eyed her like she was afraid she might choke, but made no move to help.

"They weren't actually gay," Ariana added, gaining control of her cough.

"No. Not like that. I'm saying maybe Josh killed Pearson because of a new girl."

My entire face prickled with heat. Gage smiled at my obvious discomfort.

"You're saying Josh . . . killed Thomas . . . because he wanted me?" I said, trying to keep my voice steady.

"Why not? It's not like it hasn't been done before," Gage said, leaning toward me across the table. "We all know they both wanted your body, though I, for one, never got the appeal." His cold eyes flicked over me like I was dirt. "You're nothing but trouble, New Girl. Have been ever since you got here."

"Shut up, Coolidge," Noelle said, watching my face.

"What? You can't say it isn't true. She—"

Dash brought his fist down on the table. Dishes and silverware jumped. "Back off her, man."

That was a tone no one could ignore. Gage's glee finally left him, and he dropped back in his chair like a petulant child. Everyone else slowly went back to their meals. I found myself staring at the wall clock over Gage's head, watching the second hand tick, tick, tick, until breakfast was finally over and we were released.

CRACK SECURITY

My classrooms felt smaller and grayer than usual. The tall windows looked out on a slate-gray sky, and now and then the wind would whip a tree branch against an ancient windowpane and everyone would jump. It was like we were all waiting for a bomb to drop, and why not? Every time we reached a tentative peace around this place, something huge happened to unsettle us all again. It was the status quo.

Each class that day began either with a lecture on staying the course, or a group therapy session about our feelings—all except for history. Mr. Barber being the no-nonsense type, he got right down to a review of the homework. I kept waiting for him to call on me, to try to embarrass me in front of the class. I even had a few choice comebacks all lined up. But in a rare show of compassion, the man ignored my existence.

As soon as classes let out for the day, I ran across the withering grass to Gwendolyn Hall, an old, condemned class building with crumbling stone walls and boarded-up windows. I bounded up the deteriorating steps and into the alcove in front of the door, trying not to think about the last time I'd been there—who I'd been with. Trying not to imagine spirits and ghosts and moments I could never live again. Hands shaking, I stashed my book bag under one of the benches. The place was like a cave, dark and cold—at least twenty degrees colder than the air outside. No one ever came to Gwendolyn unless it was for a quick tryst, and I had to hope that on a day like today, the make-out spot would remain deserted.

On my way out I paused for the splittest of seconds. I couldn't help it. The last time I had been here, I'd been with Thomas. Right there. Right on that bench, with his lips and his hands and his warmth. . . . God, it had been perfect then. I had been so naïve. So happy. No idea what was coming. The pointlessness of it all threatened to overwhelm me. But then I threw up a brick wall inside my mind to stay the flood. I couldn't indulge that kind of self-pity right now. I was on a mission.

Throwing the hood of my gray sweatshirt over my head, I hugged my coat close to me, looked both ways, and ran. The tall gray buildings of Easton loomed over me on all sides, glaring down at me like disapproving elders. I ignored the creeping feeling of being watched and upped the pace.

Behind the trees on the north end of the property, there was a fence. Cut out of that fence was a hole, big enough for a girl in a ball gown to crouch through. Everyone in Billings and Ketlar knew where the hole was—it had allowed us to sneak out and in on the night of the Legacy, the night all this misery had begun. I just hoped we were the only ones who knew about it. For a few long moments I was out in the open for anyone to see and snag and expel, but I refused to look anywhere but straight ahead. The dean's warnings rang in my head, but I ignored them. If someone was going to catch me, they were going to catch me on the run.

My lungs burned from the cold as I ducked through the line of trees, branches snapping at my face. I threw my back against the fence and sucked in a breath. Then I held it and listened. No air sirens, no shouting, no rabid guard dogs lusting for blood.

Walking sideways, I slowly made my way along the fence until I found the hole. Flashes from the night of the Legacy accosted me. Cold, wet feet; mud-stained skirts; Josh's hand as he helped me through. The look on his face when he'd told me they'd found Thomas. That Thomas was dead. My heart seized just thinking about it. If anyone needed proof that Josh was innocent, they needed to have been there at that moment. Unfortunately, I couldn't replicate my memory and play it for the judge and jury.

I shoved myself through the opening, caring little for the thousand-dollar coat Kiran had given me, then headed for the road. When my feet hit asphalt, I felt home free, but then I saw it, out of the corner of my eye: the media camp. At least four vans, their satellite antennae looming up into the sky. Dozens and dozens of reporters, cameramen, and various lackeys. They were all grouped around the Easton gates as if they might open at any second, like the gates of Oz, and admit them to the story of their lives.

Holding my breath, I sprinted across the street and ducked into the forest of trees on the opposite side of the road. Under cover, I made my way through piles of wet leaves and over fallen branches, the wet permeating my sneakers and soaking my socks. As I passed the crowd, I saw a man in a blue jumper perched on a ladder, affixing a security camera to a pillar at the side of the gates. The reporters shouted questions up at him.

"How do the students feel, knowing the administration has allowed a murderer to walk among them for the past few months?"

"Is there a feeling of terror on campus?"

"What are the boy's friends like? Do you believe he had any accomplices?"

These people were evil. I could only imagine the salivating they would do at my feet if I stepped into the clear and offered up my story. But that wasn't me. I didn't want a spotlight. I just wanted my boyfriend back. Half a mile up the road, I emerged onto the street again and speed-walked toward town.

The windows along Main Street in the Village of Easton glowed with welcoming warmth. Even with the cold, the streets were bustling, pairs of ladies strolled the sidewalks, popping into shops as tiny bells tinkled overhead. A woman in a black suit whisked the price-less jewelry out of the display window of one store as I passed by, getting ready to close up for the evening. She caught my eye and smiled quizzically, probably amused by the odd sight of a teenage girl in a designer coat and a tattered gray sweatshirt hood pulled tightly around her face. I ducked my head, sidestepped a couple on their way into a swank steakhouse, and kept walking toward the center of town.

VILLAGE OF EASTON, ESTABLISHED 1840. That was what the plaque on the quaint brick police station read. I stepped through the doors into a small, well-lit office, bustling with uniformed officers and detectives. I had a feeling that this was not a normal scene. That the place was usually a lot less active than this. After all, they had a murder suspect in custody. I bet no one had clocked out since they'd brought Josh through the doors. This was far too exciting for them.

Two people jumped up from chairs near the wall the moment they saw me. One shoved a tape recorder in my face.

"What's your name, Miss? Do you go to Easton Academy?"

There was a blur of movement and suddenly I was being roughly escorted toward the wall by Detective Hauer. He gave me an exasperated look and turned around, effectively blocking me from the reporters.

"Look, you two already have our official statement. You're gonna get nothing else here, so why don't you just go look under some other rock?"

The reporters scurried out, and I removed my hood and stood up straight. This was not going to be easy.

"What are you doing here, Reed?" the detective asked me. His blue shirt was wrinkled and the sleeves rolled up. There was some kind of tattoo on his forearm, but when he saw me looking, he crossed his arms over his chest.

"I want to see Josh," I told him, lifting my chin.

"I'm afraid that's not possible," he replied.

And just like that, there he was. Past Hauer's shoulder, Josh appeared. His hands were cuffed, and a woman with a severe bun and pointy features gripped his arm. They were all the way on the other side of the bullpen area, putting at least a dozen officers between him and me. It would take a miracle to get one word in, but

I had to try. I stepped aside, out from the shadow of Detective Hauer's bulk, and Josh's eyes lit up.

"Reed!"

Every cop in the place looked from him to me and back again.

"Josh! Are you all right?"

"I'm fine! I—"

"Get him out of here!" Detective Hauer bellowed, exasperated.

Josh's eyes filled with terror as the woman yanked on his arm. I took a few steps forward but was blocked by a security counter. He was just a few feet away, but I couldn't get near him. I could have clawed my way out of my skin.

"No. Wait a second!" Josh struggled away, took a step toward me. "Talk to Lewis-Hanneman and Blake! They saw me that night!" he shouted as the woman took hold of him again, this time with a lot more conviction. Lewis-Hanneman and Blake. The dean's assistant and Thomas's brother, Blake Pearson. I'd heard rumors. Was he saying the rumors were true? That they were *still* having an affair? "The art cemetery! Reed! Please! Get them to tell the truth!"

Then he was shoved through a door and the door was slammed.

That was all I needed. The slam popped a balloon inside of me, and I burst into tears.

"Come with me, Reed." The detective's voice was low and soothing and right in my ear. "Come on, kid. Come here."

My hands were over my face as I sobbed. I choked for breath. I felt his palm on my back, leading me somewhere. I fell into a chair without seeing it. Folded my arms on a table and cradled my head.

Soft words were spoken. A door opened and closed. A chair was pulled out. When I could finally breathe again, I lifted my head. My nose was so clogged I had to breathe through my mouth, and my face was tight from the tears.

"This is so wrong!" I wailed, throwing my arms out straight.

Detective Hauer was sitting across from me. He leaned forward and placed the tips of his fingers together. "Reed—"

"You can't keep him here! He didn't do anything!"

"Reed—"

"No! You have to let me talk to him," I begged. "Please!"

"Reed!"

His shout brought me up short. I sniffled and wiped under my nose with the end of my sleeve, shaking as I looked away. The detective pushed a cup of water toward me and nodded at it. I took a drink. Until that moment I hadn't realized how empty my body was.

"I'm very sorry that you're mixed up in all of this," the detective said calmly. "But you need to go back to school now. You need to try to get back to your life."

I snorted.

"Come on, you've got school. You've got your friends. Don't you have finals to study for?"

"Like any of that matters," I said.

He scooted closer to me. "You have to trust that we're doing our job. You have to trust that we're going to get this right. You need to stay out of it, Reed. For your own good."

"But . . . but what about what he just said?" I asked, sitting up.

"About Blake Pearson and the secretary from school. Were they there? Does he have an alibi?"

"We've looked into it," he said impatiently.

"And?"

"And I can't divulge any details of our investigation," he told me.

"But you have to tell me! I need to know what's—"

"We have our suspect, Reed," Hauer said through his teeth. "Don't go giving my superiors a reason to think he had an accomplice."

A cold finger of dread slid down my spine. He wasn't serious. He couldn't be.

"Now, we are going to get up and leave this office quietly," he said. "I'll drive you back to campus."

He glanced at the one window high in the wall. It was already pitch-black outside, courtesy of December.

"I don't need a ride. I'm sure it's perfectly safe," I told him, finally regaining control. I stood up and lifted my hood. "After all, you've got the big, bad killer all locked up, don't you?" I added sarcastically.

He sighed, puffing out his cheeks. Like he didn't know what to do with me. Well, he didn't have to do anything. I could take care of myself. I turned around and strode out of the room, proudly surprised that my knees didn't so much as quiver along the way.

DELETED

That night I took a long, extraordinarily hot shower, and when I emerged, my room was empty—which I had been counting on. Natasha often vacated it at about this time to go up to the roof and call her girlfriend, Leanne Shore. Her cell never worked in our room, and considering that it had started snowing and gusting about a half an hour earlier, I had to give the girl points for effort. She must have really been in love.

I needed this time to myself, to think about what Josh had said. To figure out what I was going to do next. But first things first. I dropped my towel on my bed and sat down at Natasha's computer. I had been aching to e-mail Taylor Bell ever since the night before, when her mysterious IM had been abruptly cut off. I opened up an e-mail window and typed, happy to find that my fingers were no longer trembling, as they had been since my encounter with Detective Hauer.

To: taylor_bell@gmail.com

From: rbrennan391@aol.com

Subject: IM

Don't leave me hanging, Taylor. I have to know. What
do you mean, it's all lies? Where are you? What's not
true? Please write back asap.

—Reed

I sent the e-mail, and two seconds later a new message icon
appeared on the screen. I clicked it. It was a terminal failure
message. The account taylor_bell@gmail.com had been deleted.

PROVE IT

There was this new sensation inside my chest. It had sparked up when I'd seen Josh, so helpless and alone, in the police station, and it had only grown stronger since then. Taylor's "deletion" had fueled the fire, and when I'd woken up the following morning, the feeling had taken over. It was a sort of buzzing that started deep inside my core and was now radiating outward. It was a desire to do something. To figure out what the hell was actually going on in the hallowed halls of Easton. A desire to get off my ass and fix this.

Screw Hauer. Someone had killed Thomas and it wasn't Josh. Maybe he thought it was okay to have the wrong person in jail, but I didn't. I was desperate to *do something*. I was my own person. It was time to start making my own decisions.

As my last class drew to a close the next day, I was out of my desk so fast my chair might as well have been an ejector seat. I speed-walked out of the crowded class building, nearly tripping a few people along the way, and went directly to Hell Hall. After bounding up four flights of carpeted steps, irritating several teachers and administrators along the way, I opened the door to the dean's outer office, winded like I'd just run a marathon.

Ms. Lewis-Hanneman looked up from her desk. There was an almost imperceptible twitch of her eye when she saw me. Her grip on her pen tightened. She looked small at her monstrous desk, surrounded as she was by floor-to-ceiling bookshelves packed with leather-bound books.

"The dean isn't in," she said, her tone clipped. "If you'd like to make an appointment . . ."

I stepped up to her desk and really looked at her for the first time. And for the first time, I saw it. Sure, she had the austere hairstyle and the big glasses, but add to that the blond hair, high cheekbones, and big blue eyes and she was like the saucy, repressed librarian in that fantasy that all guys seemed to harbor. No wonder Blake was attracted to her. All she had to do was take the pins out of her hair and you could cue the sexy music.

"I'm not here to see the dean," I told her. "I want to talk to you."

My heart was in my throat, but my adrenaline allowed me to take on a commanding tone, one that made Lewis-Hanneman's eyebrows arch.

"If you're selling that sinful fudge for the field hockey team, I'm not interested," she said.

I clutched the books I was still carrying to my chest. "Actually, I wanted to ask you what you were doing in Mitchell Hall the night of Thomas's murder."

Ms. Lewis-Hanneman lost all color. It was like watching a milk bottle empty. "I don't know what you're talking about."

Oh, you so *do.*

My heart pounded. She was lying right to my face. Did she not know what was at stake here?

"You don't," I challenged.

"No. I don't?" she replied. "Now, if you'd like to make an appointment to see the dean, I can arrange that for you. Otherwise, I have a lot of work to do."

Her pen shook in her grasp as she pretended to make some important note on her legal pad. I didn't move a muscle. I had gotten to her. I had this adult squirming. And I felt . . . powerful. I wondered if this was how Noelle felt every moment of every day. I stepped closer to her desk to see how much "work" she could get done with me breathing down her neck. Finally, she blew out a sigh and placed the pen on the desk.

"I believe I asked you to leave," she said firmly, looking up at me.

"I know you were there," I said, channeling Noelle. "And I know who you were with."

Let's see how you take that.

Her eyes never left my face. "Are you attempting to blackmail me, Miss Brennan?"

I blinked. Okay. So maybe I'd been thinking about blackmailing her, but just hearing her say it made me back off. That was Noelle's M.O., not mine. And I wasn't about to go there, as tempting as it was. A girl had to draw a line. Eventually.

"No. I'm asking you to just do the right thing," I said, deciding on a different tack. "If you have an alibi for Josh Hollis, you have to go to the police. This is his whole life we're talking about here."

She held my gaze for a long moment. There was a second in which I saw the pity in her eyes. Saw that she knew what I was dealing with here. Knew how scared I was. In that second I was sure she was going to agree with me, but it passed as quickly as it had come.

"Miss Brennan, I already told the police everything I know, which is exactly nothing," she said coolly. "I was at home by myself that night. My husband was away on business, and he and I spoke on the phone. That is the extent of my memory of that night."

"You're lying," I spat.

"At the risk of sounding like a five-year-old here, Miss Brennan . . . prove it."

I wanted to smack her across the face. Pull her hair out. Rip her glasses off and throw them at the wall. But at that moment, the door opened and the dean walked in, and I never had the chance to find out if I was actually capable of such a tantrum.

"Miss Brennan," Dean Marcus said, surprised to see me. He removed his tweed hat and held it before him. "How are you?"

I took a step back from Ms. Lewis-Hanneman's desk. Putting some distance between us seemed to assuage the need to hurt her.

"I'm all right," I said, my voice quaking.

He looked at me as if I was some foreign creature. Something he was wary of approaching. Should he hold his hand out under my nose so I could sniff him out, or would I bite?

THESE ARE MY FRIENDS

I needed Noelle. That much was clear. The more I thought about it, the more certain I was that she would have gotten the truth out of Ms. Lewis-Hanneman. She wouldn't have backed off. She wouldn't have stopped until she'd gotten what she wanted. I couldn't do the things Noelle could do. Maybe that was a bad thing. Maybe it was a good thing. I hadn't entirely decided yet. But at least in the meantime I had the girl who was capable of anything in my corner.

At least, I was pretty sure I did.

As I walked across the frigid campus toward Billings House that night, I had to wonder. Yes, Noelle had been a good friend to me. At least, she had since we'd gotten past the Walt Whittaker double-blackmail debacle. All she had done was try to protect me. There was no denying that her methods had been somewhat questionable, but that was just Noelle. Whatever her tactics, her motives always seemed clear. She wanted to keep her friends from making mistakes. She wanted to make sure we were on the right path. And she would do pretty much anything to ensure that we stayed out of trouble.

But then there was Taylor. She'd told me I couldn't trust the other Billings Girls. That they had been lying to me. But about what? And why? Had they only lied about Taylor's reasons for leaving, or was it bigger than that? And if they had lied about Taylor, then where was she, and why had she left school? Maybe I should start by confronting Noelle about that. I deserved to know the truth, after all. Taylor was my friend. They were all supposed to be my friends. So why was I always the only one in the dark?

I stopped outside the front door of the dorm. In the distance a siren wailed—the town of Easton's fire siren. I listened to the sound echoing through the bare trees.

Did I really need Noelle's help? I knew Lewis-Hanneman was lying. Maybe I should just try to break her myself. But how? I didn't even know where to start. Begging? Back to blackmailing? No. She'd already seen me back off of that option. She'd know I was bluffing. That I was too weak. And this was Josh's life we were talking about here. I couldn't afford to mess this up.

Noelle would know what to do. Noelle would get results. Noelle was my only option.

Finally resolved, I grasped the cold door handle and walked into Billings.

"We have less than three weeks left until finals and he wants to keep us caged up in here like we're animals? As far as I'm concerned, he's just asking for trouble."

Noelle. Her voice as authoritative as ever. I paused in the entry-way. The lobby area was deserted. Noelle was holding court in the parlor to my right.

"But you heard what he said," Cheyenne Martin replied. I recognized her voice by its superior tone. "We have to stick together right now. For Easton."

"Screw Easton," Noelle said.

Cheyenne actually gasped, and I bit back a laugh.

"All I'm saying is, we should do what we always do this time of year," Noelle said.

"Party!" one of the Twin Cities called out. I wasn't sure if it was London or Vienna, but it didn't make much difference: They pretty much shared the same brain. I felt a curl of black anger winding its way around my heart as a few of the other girls laughed and shouted. That's what they were discussing? Sneaking off campus to party? Did no one understand what was going on around here?

"Exactly," Noelle said. "Don't we deserve to let off some steam after the semester we've had? It's been one downer after another."

Downer? That was how she was classifying Thomas's disappearance? His death? Josh's arrest? As *downers*?

"I say we get the hell out of here," Noelle continued, apparently sensing that the girls were aligning with her. "Have a little fun. Try not to think about all the . . . unpleasantness."

"Yeah."

"Sounds good to me."

"What's the dean going to do, anyway? Expel us?"

I felt weak with anger. These were my friends. The people I had wanted so badly to be with. What the hell was wrong with me?

"That's exactly what he's going to do," Cheyenne piped up. "Listen, girls, I understand that you want to get your minds off everything. Everyone on this campus does. But those people are out there just waiting to write another story about how hedonistic all us private school kids are—"

"Hedonistic. Big word," Kiran joked. "Trying to bring up that SAT verbal, Shy?"

"I'm serious, *Kir*," Cheyenne said. "Do you really want to give them what they want?"

Noelle snorted a laugh. "You were born in the wrong generation, Martin."

"Or maybe I was just born with a conscience," Cheyenne replied. "I say if you want a night to chill, we do it here. We'll have a nice, casual, sophisticated soiree right here in Billings. The dean can't object to that, and we'll all just be able to kick back and relax."

"Okay, Carol Brady. You do that, and the rest of us will have some real fun," Noelle said.

"R-rated fun," Kiran added. "Illegal substances, adult language—"

"Maybe even some sexual content," Noelle put in.

The room filled with cackling laughter and something inside of me snapped. I stormed over to the doorway and, since there was no other way to make my presence known, dropped my book bag on the floor with a thud. Everyone turned to look at me.

"What the hell is wrong with you people?" I shouted.

Noelle stepped forward. "Reed—"

"No. You're talking about *partying* right now? When one of your friends is dead and another one is sitting in jail for his murder? Oh, yeah! This is cause for celebration, people! Let's go into the city and get R-rated!"

Kiran scoffed and looked away. No one else moved.

"I don't know about you people, but this kind of . . . of *horrifying* thing doesn't happen every day in my world!"

"It doesn't happen in ours either," Ariana said quietly.

I grabbed my bag and glared at her. "Well, you wouldn't know it."

"We didn't do anything, Reed," Kiran blurted suddenly, standing.

"Kiran," Ariana said.

"No! I'm so sick of this. We're not the ones who did in your little boyfriend, Reed," Kiran snapped. "Josh did. Your precious Josh. But you walk around here being all accusatory all the time. Like we did something wrong. Well, guess what? We didn't do anything!"

"Maybe not," I said calmly. "But *someone* did, and you're acting like you're perfectly okay with it. And that's what I'm mad about."

For once, no one tried to stop me and talk me down when I turned to go.

ON MY OWN

Hands shaking, I pulled my cell phone out of my bag. I couldn't believe I was about to do what I was about to do, but if I was going to, I had to do it now, before I lost my nerve. Before the angry adrenaline surge fizzled and died.

I scrolled through my contacts until the icon landed on "Thomas." A bubble welled up in the back of my throat. I wouldn't even have this option if it wasn't for him. For that playful night when he'd programmed his numbers into my phone, saying he wanted me to be able to get ahold of him wherever, whenever. Like we would always be together. Like we might have been, if not for . . .

I closed my eyes and swallowed. I had to focus. I had to be strong. This was for Josh *and* for Thomas. I highlighted the home number. I had thought about deleting this so many times but just hadn't been able to bring myself to do it. Now I was glad I'd been so sentimental. I pressed "send."

The phone was cold against my ear. I hugged myself and sat on the edge of my bed.

"Pearson residence."

The voice was clipped. Slightly accented. Something European.

"Yes, may I speak to Blake, please?" I squeaked.

"I'm sorry, but Blake is away at school just now."

"Oh, right." Of course, Reed. You think a guy like Blake Pearson doesn't go to college? "Can I . . . uh . . . get that number?"

"I'm sorry, but I'm not at liberty to divulge that information," the woman said, with a laugh in her voice.

"Right. Right. Of course. Well, could I—"

"Good evening."

She hung up the phone. I threw the cell down on the bed and went to Natasha's computer. If I could find out which college Blake attended, maybe the school's information system would give me his number.

I searched for "Blake Pearson." Thousands of results appeared. Blake Pearson was a more common name than I ever would have thought. Blake was an artist, a businessman, a lawyer, a dancer. Blake was everywhere.

I started to crash from my adrenaline high. This was pointless. Did I really think I could do something? That I could effect some change? Feeling utterly defeated, I sat back in the desk chair. Just as my shoulders started to roll forward, there was a rap on the door and it opened.

Noelle. At least she had knocked.

"Nice drama back there. You been watching too much Telenova?" she asked, crossing her arms over her chest.

"Did you want something?" I spat.

Her eyebrow arched. "Not that I owe you any explanations, but I wanted you to know that I wasn't trying to be callous. All I want to do is help everyone decompress. And from the way you're acting, I think you might need one night of distraction more than anyone."

My jaw clenched of its own accord.

"I'm only thinking of you," she added.

As always. My protector. My savior. I was beginning to think it was nothing but a line. And yet, part of me still wanted to ask her for help. All I had to do was open my mouth and ask and she'd tell me exactly where Blake went to college. But if I did that, she'd want to know why I wanted to know. She'd be part of this, and at that moment I didn't much like her, let alone trust her. At that moment the only person I trusted was myself.

"I'd really like to be alone right now," I said.

"Reed, come on. I just want things to go back to normal around here. Don't you just want to feel normal again?"

"Well, maybe that's the difference between you and me, Noelle. Because for me, as long as Josh is locked up somewhere for something he didn't do, I don't think anything's ever going to feel normal."

She stared at me for a moment, then laughed in the back of her throat, tipped her head forward, and covered her face with her hands. Embarrassed? At a loss? Was it even possible? But when she looked up again, pushing her hair back from her face with her hands, she was perfectly composed.

"Could you be any more high-and-mighty?" she said.

"You invented the concept."

Whoa. Had I really just said that? From the look on her face, Noelle couldn't believe it either.

"No one talks to me like that."

My heart was on the verge of stopping completely. I ignored it. "Well, there's a first time for everything."

"Fine. When you decide to stop acting like a child, I'll be in my room."

And then I was alone again.

AN ALLY

There was a little part of me that thought Noelle was right. At least in one respect. Getting the hell off the Easton campus *would* be a nice change of pace. Especially since being around people at all and the Billings Girls in particular was making me extremely tense. They were just so . . . very willing to accept that the whole thing was over and to put it behind them. It made me want to scream. Or knock their heads together. Or perhaps get up and overturn the cafeteria table where we all sat for each and every meal.

I stood at the end of that table, which was, for the moment, deserted, and considered sitting somewhere else. I had left the dorm fifteen minutes early just so that I wouldn't have to walk with them to dinner, but even in my current volatile state, I knew that not sitting at Noelle's table would be an affront worse than wearing last year's shoes, which was pretty much unforgivable. But I could sit all the way down here, at the opposite end from where they usually sat. I could separate myself that much.

I took my seat and pulled out my copy of *The Invisible Man*. This was me, engrossed in my studies. This was me, too busy to talk.

After a short while the cafeteria began to fill up with people. As always their conversations became hushed as they passed by me. As always I could feel the stares on the back of my neck. I simply kept my eyes trained on my book and read the same sentence for the tenth time.

My mind wandered to Thomas. Snapshots of him, lying dead. I winced. Tried to clear my mind. For the past few weeks I had tried to avoid thinking about the details of how he'd died, but every once in a while I couldn't stop my imagination from conjuring these images. I couldn't stop. . . .

The bat. Someone had used Josh's baseball bat to bash Thomas's head in. The blood, the tears, the begging, the sound of wood hitting. . . .

Suddenly I was gasping for breath.

Okay. Fine. I was fine. It was over. Done. It was going to be fine. Fine, fine, fine.

Soon I heard the approach of the girls. Noelle. Ariana. Kiran. Not Taylor, because she was God knows where doing God knows what. Gage's voice was louder than anyone else's. I breathed in through my nose, out through my mouth. In through my nose, out through my mouth.

The chair across from me was pulled out, which startled me. I looked up. It was only Natasha. She gave me an understanding, encouraging look and silently went about her business.

Noelle, Ariana, and Kiran settled in at their end of the table, chatting as if nothing was amiss. London and Vienna defected from the next table over and filled in the seats between us. I looked at my book. Really concentrated this time. Read the sentence for the twentieth time. I was just settling into a cautious level of relative comfort when Dash made his entrance.

"You guys are not going to believe this bullshit," he said, yanking a chair out from another table and slamming it down at the end of ours. His cheeks were blotched with cold and anger and his blond hair was mussed. He did not sit down. "They're keeping Josh locked up on charges of withholding evidence."

A cold sweat slipped over my body. Withholding evidence. Hadn't I done the same thing when I hadn't shown them Thomas's final note? Were they coming for me next?

"They don't have enough to charge him with murder, so they're claiming he didn't divulge important information," Dash continued, throwing his arms out. "They're making this up as they go along."

Everyone looked at everyone else, but no one spoke.

"I'll bite," Natasha said finally. "What important information?"

"They say he should have reported his bat missing," Dash spat. "Can you believe that crap?"

"Are you kidding me?" Gage asked. "I lost a pen that day— should I report *that*?"

"Dash, how did you find out about this?" Noelle asked.

"My dad. He's working with Josh's lawyer and his parents. They

got in from Germany yesterday morning. Freaking out, of course."
He took a deep breath and blew it out. "Isn't this, like, unconstitu-
tional or something?" he asked, looking at Natasha.

"I . . . no. Not exactly," she said. "I mean, as far as I know, as
long as they charge him with something—"

"But what if that something is completely transparent?" Dash
blurted, like Natasha was the bad guy. "What the hell kind of system
is this? We have to *do* something."

At that moment I recognized in Dash everything I had been feeling myself. I was just opening my mouth to agree with him when—

"What do you want them to do? Let him go so he can come back
here and kill somebody else?" Ariana asked.

Silence fell. The cold sheen of sweat froze into a skin of ice.

"Reed—"

I don't even know who said my name. I had already shoved my
chair back from the table and left.

IN BUSINESS

After spending the rest of dinner in the infirmary, I went directly to the library. I had three hours before I had to be back at my dorm. Three hours to figure out what to do next.

I stepped into the hushed warmth of the Easton library. The brown-and-gray marble floor gleamed, and the gold-glass lights cast a dim glow over the airy lobby. Instantly, the scent of musty books enveloped me, soothing my frazzled nerves. The elderly librarian at the checkout desk, with his suede-capped sleeves and thick glasses, didn't look up from his work. I breathed a bit easier.

Slipping by the desk, I tugged my scarf from the collar of my coat and headed for the European history section. I heard a few whispers and hesitated. Who could possibly have gotten here before me? Whoever it was sat on the other side of the stacks. I resolved to stare straight ahead and stride right past them. Which I did, but I couldn't help looking out of the corner of my eye.

No one I knew. Three freshmen. Poring over the student news-paper, the *Easton Academy Chronicle*. The headline read STUDENTS BACK TO WORK AFTER THANKSGIVING BREAK. A real gripper. Part of the dean's let's-play-happy mandate. Disgusted, I kept right on walk-ing, but then it hit me.

The student newspaper. Back home in Croton, the final issue of the high school paper always listed all of the graduating seniors and their future plans—which colleges they were attending, whether they were going right to work or to a trade school. Would the *Easton Academy Chronicle* do the same? I laughed over the fact that I could doubt it for even a second. Of course they would. They would want to show off the percentage of Ivy League spots they'd won. If I could just get my hands on the last paper from Blake's graduation year . . .

I turned around and strode back to the front desk. The librarian languidly turned a yellowing page in his book.

"Excuse me?"

He sighed and continued to read. I tensed up.

"Excuse me. I just have a quick question."

He lifted one craggy finger and the clock behind him tick, tick, ticked. I held my breath.

"I'm sorry, I—"

He lifted his head. Trained his perfectly clear and alert eyes on me.

"Yes, Miss? I've finished my page now," he said calmly. "What, might I ask, is so urgent?"

Okay, Reed. Chill. This man deals with obnoxious, over-privileged kids all day long. He has every right to finish his page before he helps you. Of course, if he knew that someone's life was at stake here . . .

But never mind.

"I was just wondering if you keep old copies of the student newspaper?" I asked.

"Yes, we do. They're on the front shelf in the history section, bound by year." He returned to his book, and I hightailed it to the far wall of the library, my heart pounding like a jackhammer.

There they were, right at eye level: dozens of brown, leather-bound volumes with gold lettering. EASTON ACADEMY CHRONICLE, 1964–1965. I ran my hand along the books until I found the year I was looking for and yanked the tome down. In the back was that year's graduation issue, and right inside the front page was the list.

My eyes ran down the alphabetical names, looking for the P's, but even in my haste, I couldn't help noticing the ridiculously elite list of schools. Harvard, Yale, Princeton, Oxford, Sarah Lawrence, Stanford, the Sorbonne. Back home the list pretty much went Penn State, Penn State, Pitt, Penn State, vocational school. . . . I felt an incongruent flutter of pride that I was part of this place, then remembered instantly all the total misery and insanity this place had brought down on me. I found the P's.

"Blake Pearson . . . Columbia University."

Excitement rushed through me. I'd done it. All on my own. Who needed Noelle and her questionable methods? I could handle this myself.

I slammed the book shut and headed for the computer lab near the stacks. All I needed was Blake's e-mail address at Columbia and I was in business.

SHOT IN THE DARK

To: BlPearson@columbia.edu
From: rbrennan391@aol.com
Subject: A request

Dear Blake,

I don't know if you know who I am. Your brother, Thomas, and I were dating just before he died. I know it must be difficult for you to hear about what happened—it is for me—so I won't dwell on it. I'll just say I'm sorry.

As you probably know, Thomas's good friend Josh Hollis has been arrested for his murder. I know that Josh didn't do it, and I think you do too. Josh told me that you were here at Easton that night and that maybe you could give him an alibi. I guess I'm writing this e-mail to ask you to call the police and let them know.

I can't stand that Josh is in jail for something he didn't do, and I'm sure you wouldn't want Thomas's friend to suffer either.

Please call them. Or call me. Or if you do call them, let me know. I'm sorry if this sounds pushy or whatever, but I didn't know what else to do. You have my e-mail. My cell phone number is (914) 555-9113. You can call me or text me there. I hope to hear from you soon. And again, I'm so sorry for your loss.

Sincerely,

Reed Brennan

A BILLINGS CHRISTMAS

"Oh my God, I cannot wait to get to Bali," Kiran grumbled, as another gust of wind sprayed us with freezing rain. It was the day after my dramatic dinner walkout, and I was trying to act semi-normal to keep Noelle and the others from constantly telling me to get over it and move on. Part of that meant walking from the cafeteria back to the dorm with them after tonight's meal, but I made sure that Kiran and Noelle were between myself and Ariana. Because every time I thought about that last comment Ariana had made about Josh, I wanted to strangle her. And the last thing any of us needed right now was more violence.

It had been spritzing on and off all day, and now that the sun had gone down, the rain felt ten times colder. It was like being blasted in the face with frozen buckshot—or what I imagine that might feel like.

"I'm warm," Kiran said, closing her eyes momentarily. "I'm warm and I'm on the beach, sipping a margarita and watching my skin darken. . . ."

"Nothing like Christmas on the equator," Noelle said with a sigh. "Did I tell you I convinced my parents to get me my own villa?"

"I think the Lange family is responsible for half the gross national income of St. Bart's each year," Kiran joked.

I pulled out my cell phone and checked the screen for the four hundredth time today. No calls. No text messages. I'd e-mailed Blake from the library almost twenty-four hours ago with my number and e-mail address, and nothing. Was it possible he hadn't gotten the e-mail yet, or was he just plain ignoring me?

"It's worth it if I don't have to pretend I don't see the 'rents sneaking in their sloppy sides and thinking they're getting away with it," Noelle said.

"Sloppy sides?" I said, trying to focus on something else.

"Yeah. Their side dishes. They both put their significant others up at hotels on the island every year," Noelle told me, looking right into my eyes with no shame whatsoever. For the first time all year, she was wearing a hat. It was gray wool and pulled low over her forehead and ears. With her cashmere scarf up over her nose, all that was visible were her eyes and perfect lashes. "Wallace and Claire really give new meaning to the phrase 'Ho, ho, ho.'"

Huh. Apparently Noelle's life was not, in fact, perfect outside of Easton. That was the first I'd heard of it. But it didn't seem like she cared much, or at all.

"Don't you guys sort of miss out on the decorations and the music and everything?" I asked, deciding to change the subject.

The Christmas season was the only time of the year my hometown could actually pass as pretty, with all the lights and trees and wreaths decorating the strip malls and town buildings. I almost liked it this time of year. Not that I was looking forward to returning. Inside the Brennan home it was always dreary, no matter what was going on outside.

"Who needs strings of lights when you can have string bikinis?" Kiran replied.

"And trust me, a mai-tai is much more festive than eggnog," Noelle added.

"I'm with Reed," Ariana announced, putting a chill right through me. "For me, there's nothing like a cozy fire and a big fir tree and being surrounded by people who love you."

"A fire? In Atlanta?" Kiran asked.

"It can get pretty cold there," Ariana said, her blue eyes—usually so piercing—alive with light. "I love this time of year."

"Well, I honestly don't care where I go as long as I get the hell out of here," Kiran said as we reached the front door of Billings. "This place is *de*-pressing."

We walked inside. The first things that hit me were the scents of cinnamon, mulberry, and freshly baked cookies. The next was the incredible, musky warmth. We all paused and then quickly shoved ourselves through the inner door.

"Whoa," I said, nearly tripping over a faux-fur rug that had not been there that morning.

In fact, there were a lot of things that hadn't been there that morning: the huge Christmas tree in the corner, decorated with white lights, red ribbons, and gold ornaments. The fir garland, peppered with acorns and red flowers, strung from the fireplace, the banister, and every doorway. The dozens and dozens of red and white poinsettias. The hundreds of tapered candles in crystal stems. The huge logs alight in the fireplace. And the three waiters in tuxedos, passing champagne, eggnog, hors d'oeuvres, and cookies on silver platters. The *Nutcracker Suite* was being played by a string quartet made up of Easton students, and all the Billings Girls were dressed up in velvet and cashmere and pearls, circulating around the room with the boys of Ketlar, who had donned business casual for the occasion.

It was a Hallmark card come to life.

"What the hell?" Noelle blurted, ripping off her hat and scarf.

Rose Sakowitz strolled by, her curly red hair back in a black headband to match her slim, sleeveless dress. I grabbed her skinny wrist, and she nearly spilled her mug of hot chocolate all over the new rug.

"You can just say, 'Hey, you,' Reed. You don't have to grab me," she said good-naturedly.

"Sorry. I think I'm in shock. What is all this?" I asked.

"Ask Cheyenne," Rose replied with a grin. "She's been working on it for days. I think she's petitioning to be the next Martha Stewart."

"Where the hell did she get all this stuff?" Noelle asked.

"The Internet," Rose said proudly. "She ordered it all, then spent half the afternoon decorating. Plus she paid some of the staff from the cafeteria to stay late and wait, since she wasn't allowed to hire an outside caterer to come on campus. Genius, isn't it?"

I was inclined to agree. Already the aromatherapy was working its wonders on my coiled shoulder muscles. Noelle, however, was practically spitting fire. Cheyenne had pitched this idea the other day, and Noelle had shot it down, but Cheyenne had gone ahead with it anyway. In the Billings universe, that was heresy.

"Isn't this incredible?" London trilled, bounding over. Her huge breasts were all but popping out of her red sweater, and she wore a Santa hat at a jaunty angle atop her thick, wavy hair. "We couldn't go out, so Cheyenne brought Christmas in!"

"God, how lame," Kiran said, even as she grabbed a champagne flute from a passing waiter.

Noelle had heard enough. She flung her coat over the back of one of the couches that had been moved to the lobby from the parlor and stormed into the next room. Of course, Kiran, Ariana, Rose, and I had to follow. The parlor was decorated much like the lobby, and *White Christmas* was playing on the big-screen TV. Dash stepped away from the wall to greet Noelle, but she blew right by him and zeroed in on Cheyenne. She stood near the wall with a tall guy from Ketlar named Trey, her diamond studs sparkling in the candlelight. She wore a white turtleneck, a plaid skirt, and a black velvet headband just like Rose's. Girl could have stepped right out of a Burberry ad.

"Cheyenne—"

"Noelle!" Cheyenne said with a big smile. "What do you think?"

"I think it looks like Rudolph threw up in here," Noelle replied.

Cheyenne's smile faltered, but only for a moment. "Well, every-one has their own taste, I suppose."

"Let's skip the pleasantries, Rachael Ray. What the hell do you think you're doing planning this behind my back?" Noelle demanded.

Trey took a step closer to Cheyenne. Brave guy. Most would have backed away.

"I didn't realize that every little thing we did in the dorm had to be approved by you," Cheyenne said tersely. "I mean, I know you like to throw your weight around, but there's no president of Billings, is there? Not officially."

I thought Noelle was going to rupture something. Kiran chuckled under her breath.

"And besides, I knew you thought it was a bad idea, and I also knew that everyone else would enjoy it. And look," Cheyenne con-tinued, lifting her hands. "They do."

"That's because they're drunk," Noelle said flatly.

"If you say so," Cheyenne replied. Dear Lord. Was that conde-scension? Did this girl have some kind of preppy death wish? "Now can I please get back to my date?"

Cheyenne turned toward Trey, but Noelle didn't move. Her eyes narrowed as she worked something out. Then she slowly smiled, and I felt pity for Cheyenne.

"I thought you were dating Ennis Thatcher from Barton School," Noelle said finally.

Cheyenne's shimmery lips slowly twisted into a smirk. "Well, I couldn't exactly invite him, considering the restrictions, could I? Besides, unlike you, Noelle, I'm not ball-and-chained to my man. I do what I like."

"I'm not ball-and-chained to anyone," Noelle fumed. As if on cue, Dash stepped up behind her and slipped his arm around her waist.

"Hey, babe," he said, clearly already buzzed on champagne. Otherwise he never would have used the word "babe." Noelle slapped his hand away.

Cheyenne all but laughed. "My mistake."

"So are you not at all concerned that Ennis might find out about this?" Kiran asked Cheyenne, finishing off her champagne. She eyed Trey up and down. "Not that I question your taste."

"Why? It's not like anyone here is going to tell him," Cheyenne said blithely, lifting one shoulder. "Billings Girls protect their own, right?"

The girl wasn't fazed. Frustrated, Noelle turned around and headed back toward the lobby.

"This party is a joke," she said under her breath. "Come on, Dash. Let's go up to my room."

Dash, even with everything that was going on, didn't have to be told twice. He dropped his glass on a bookshelf and went after his girl.

"Where'd you get that hot chocolate?" I asked Rose.

She smiled. "It's in the other room. There are even mini marshmallows."

"I love mini marshmallows," I told her. "Let's go."

Ariana and Kiran looked baffled as Rose and I left them behind, but I didn't even care. Maybe they all thought this was lame, but to me, it was heaven. In the lobby I filled a red mug with steaming cocoa and covered the top with a generous heap of marshmallows. Then I grabbed a few sugar cookies and joined Natasha over by the fire. Rose settled in next to me and I let the chocolatey goodness warm me from the inside out. For the first time in days I felt semi-relaxed, and I was going to enjoy it for as long as humanly possible.

When Cheyenne strolled through the room a few minutes later, I reached up and touched her hand. She looked down at me, surprised. Not that I could blame her—ever since she'd crushed her blush beads into her rug and made me clean it up during my hazing stage, there had been no love lost between the two of us. But as of tonight I was seeing Cheyenne in a whole different light.

"Thanks for this," I said.

Cheyenne smiled kindly, and I felt that in that moment, any leftover animosity between us was erased. "You're welcome."

FRUSTRATION

The next day the clouds and rain were gone, leaving a crisp blue sky in their wake. First thing in the morning I got out of bed, taking my comforter with me to guard against the cold, and padded over to Natasha's desk. She snored lightly in her bed as I powered up her computer. My fingers trembled both with anticipation and from the chill as I logged on to my e-mail. He had to have responded by now. He just had to.

I logged on. My breath caught. There was one new message. I clicked to my inbox. The message was from my brother. I groaned and opened it.

To: rbrennan391@aol.com
From: Scott.Brennan@PAState.edu
Subject: Whaddup, loser? And other burning questions.

Hey. So. I'm not gonna be able to make the drive out with Dad to pick you up. I have a final that last day.

Bastards. Sorry. Really wanted to get a firsthand look at Eat Me Academy. How are things there? Any more normal? Hope you're hanging in. Know you are. You're tough like that.

All right. Enough with the mush. Call me later, loser.

Scott

I sighed and typed a response.

To: Scott.Brennan@PAState.edu
From: rbrennan391@aol.com
Subject: You're a jackass. And other lame responses.

Wanna know how things are here? I can't wait to get home. What does that tell you?
—Reed

As soon as I sent it, I checked my inbox again. As if Blake would be up at 6 a.m. typing notes to his dead brother's girlfriend. Nothing. I bit my tongue and went back to bed to lie there and stare at the ceiling. At seven I got up, checked my e-mail again, cursed under my breath, and took a shower.

For the rest of the day I was a sweaty mess. That's what happens when you spend the ten minutes in between each class sprinting to the library to check your e-mail, finding nothing, and then sprinting back again. With each fruitless venture I grew more and more frustrated, both at Blake for not replying, and at myself for continuing to believe that he would. Finally, on my last try between my final class and dinner, I sent him another e-mail. I had to retype several of the words over and over again, my hands were shaking so badly.

To: BlPearson@columbia.edu
From: rbrennan391@aol.com
Subject: Your conscience

Dear Blake,

How do you live with yourself, knowing that an innocent person is sitting in jail and all you have to do is pick up the phone to fix it? Now I understand why Thomas hated you so much.

Regards,
Reed

I regretted it the moment I hit "send." Telling someone off like that was probably not the best way to coerce them into cooperating. But there was nothing I could do about it now. The message was out there. I just had to hope it pissed Blake off enough for him to call me and scream at me. Then at least I'd have a shot at talking to him.

JOINING FORCES

The next day there was still nothing from Blake. Not even a "screw you" text message. I considered going back to talk to Ms. Lewis-Hanneman, but I had no idea what I could say to make her talk. Blake seemed like the more viable option. He had nothing to lose by divulging that he'd been on campus. No one would care if he was having an affair with a staff member. He wouldn't get in trouble. And he had everything to gain. Even if he and Thomas did dislike each other, they were still brothers. Wouldn't Blake want the real killer to be found? Someone had to get through to him, and clearly it was not going to be me. Who did I know who knew Blake? Who might actually be able to get him on the phone and talk some sense into him?

As soon as I had this thought, the answer was blatantly clear. I found Dash studying for his advanced chemistry exam in the library. Unfortunately, he was not alone. Gage was with him, snapping his gum and listening to his iPod as he studied the physique of some Swedish model in the latest issue of *Maxim*. Cheyenne's boy toy, Trey Prescott, was there as well, scribbling notes onto index cards. This was going to be interesting. I'd never talked to Dash on my own before.

I stepped up to their table and cleared my throat. Dash and Trey looked up.

"Hey," I said.

"What's up?" Dash asked.

"Could I . . . uh . . . talk to you?" I asked, looking uncertainly at Gage. He still hadn't noticed me. Thank goodness for those deafening earbuds.

Dash was clearly intrigued. He pushed away from the table. "Sure."

As he stood, Gage did look up. He popped the buds from his ears. "What's going on?"

"Nothing, man. Just stay," Dash said. Like Gage was a dog. Gage looked irritated for a moment but sighed and put his buds back in. Good boy. "Over here," Dash told me.

He touched my back and steered me to the alcove with the Evian and candy vending machines. The fluorescent light overhead flickered as we leaned against opposite walls of the small doorway. Even with my tall and athletic build, Dash dwarfed me. His broad shoulders pulled the sleeves of his blue sweater taut, and he had to be at least six foot four.

"What's wrong? Is it Josh?" Dash whispered.

"No. Well, sort of." I took a deep breath and looked into Dash's guileless eyes. I hoped I was doing the right thing. I thought that I was. I plowed ahead. "It turns out he has an alibi."

Dash's face lit up and he stood straight. "He does! That's great!"

"Yeah, but neither of the people who saw him that night will come forward," I told him.

"Who are they?" Dash asked.

"Blake Pearson and Ms. Lewis-Hanneman."

Dash reached both hands up and held them over his mouth as though he were praying. "You've got to be kidding me. They're still at it?"

"Apparently. But she's lying about it, and he won't return my e-mails," I told him. "They were in Mitchell Hall that night, and Josh went there. He hangs out in the art cemetery sometimes when Thomas gets . . . got . . . you know . . ."

"Wasted," Dash said, clenching his jaw.

"Yeah." I looked away. I could hear a few girls whispering nearby but couldn't tell if they were getting closer.

"So you've tried to get in touch with Blake?" Dash asked.

"Yeah, but nothing."

"Asshole." Dash crossed his arms over his chest, and his perfect brows knitted as he paced to the vending machines and back again. "Okay, I think I know a way we can get Blake's ass up here so we can talk to him in person."

"You do? How?" I asked, my heart starting to pound.

"We have to use Lewis-Hanneman. Blake would do anything for

that woman," he told me. "Although I don't know why. She always seemed like a frigid bitch to me."

A lot of people would have described his girlfriend the same way, but I refrained from pointing that out.

"I told you, she won't help."

"Doesn't matter. We just need to figure out how to get into Hell Hall after hours." Dash paused in front of me, racking his brain.

"Oh, I know a way," I said, preening just slightly. I had, after all, been forced to break in there a couple of months ago in the dead of night. I could do it again, no problem.

"You do?" Dash asked.

"Piece of cake," I said. "When do you want to do it?"

"As soon as possible," he replied, psyched to have a clear task at hand. "Tonight."

"Okay, meet me there at—"

"Well, well! What's this? Should I be concerned?"

Noelle strolled over to us, still in her coat. I felt all the blood rush to my face and took a step away from Dash. Couldn't have been more obviously guilty if I'd had the word stamped across my chest. Dash's eyes met mine and I shook my head ever so slightly.

"Dash was just giving me some pointers for my modern civ project," I said quickly.

"Really?" Noelle arched her brows at her boyfriend.

I silently prayed that he would go along with my story, not thinking for a second that he would. They were Dash and Noelle, after all—the perfect couple against which all other perfect couples were

measured. If she found out what I knew she would certainly inter-
fere.

"Yeah," Dash said, slipping his arm over her shoulders. "You
know how much Kline loves me."

My jaw dropped in surprise, but I quickly snapped it shut. If
Noelle noticed, she didn't let on.

"How very generous of you," she said to Dash. "Reed could use a
little help, considering all she's been through."

"Yeah. That's what I figured," Dash said with a grin.

"Thanks again for all your ideas," I told him, edging away. "I
think I'll go get started on the research."

Noelle kissed Dash on the lips, then hugged him, turning her
back to me. As I stepped away, Dash wrapped his arms around her
but looked at me.

Midnight, he mouthed.

My heart skipped an excited beat and I nodded before quickly
walking away. My palms itched like crazy as I grabbed my books and
made my way to the computer lab. For now I would try to get some
actual work done on that project—both to keep up appearances and
maybe even save my grade. But I could hardly wait for later tonight
when I would break and enter for the second time since arriving at
Easton. For the first time, I was grateful for my Billings hazing
period. At least some of it was about to be put to good use.

DOUBLE-O DASH

We had to be out of our minds, because breaking into Hell Hall in the middle of the night after cameras had been installed all over campus and the security staff had been doubled? Not too smart.

Still, I didn't even think about turning back as I snuck out of Billings House that night. I had long since learned that the back stairs were far less squeaky than the front (this from many nights of listening to my sister Billings Girls tromp up and down, in and out), so I tiptoed down the hall, past Noelle and Ariana's room, and held the door of the stairwell until it clicked closed quietly. Then I jogged downstairs on my tiptoes, crossed the deserted lobby, and paused by the door. Already I could feel the biting grasp of the winter night. I lifted the hood of my black hoodie, buttoned up my black coat, and slipped out into the cold.

The moment I was outside, I ducked my head and ran. My white sneakers cut an eerie streak through the pitch-black night. No stars. No moon. The weather had cooperated with our scheme by giving us serious cloud cover. Still, I sprinted as fast as I could. By the time I reached Hell Hall, my lungs burned from the frigid air and I really had to pee. Nerves. They do it to me every time.

"I'm here," Dash whispered, stepping out of the shadows.

I could have laughed when I saw him. Black turtleneck with a little *RL* embroidered into the neck. Black skullcap by A/X. Flat front, black wool pants. Very high-end skulker. Did the wealthy have a catalog for everything?

"You sure you want to do this?" I asked. He was, after all, God's gift to Easton. This type of thing could be bad for the golden boy's reputation. I, however, couldn't tarnish mine much more without a blowtorch.

Dash nodded resolutely. "I'm sure. Whatever happens is worth it if it helps Josh."

I smiled. This guy was so pure he practically glowed. I hoped he never went into politics. He'd get slaughtered. Or just corrupted, which would be sad. My heartbeat started to return to normal, which made me feel ready for the next step.

"Okay," I said. "This way."

I crept along the stone wall of Hell Hall until I found the basement window, the one that had slid open so easily the last time I'd committed this particular infraction. Back then, I'd been stealing a test for Ariana. A test it turned out she didn't even need. The memory tasted bitter in my mouth. If I'd known then what I knew now. Where all of this would lead . . . Well, I couldn't think about that now. I crouched next to the pane and Dash followed, breaking a couple dozen azalea branches with his bulk. I slid the window open.

"That was absurdly easy," Dash said.

We both stared at the three-by-three-foot opening.

"Physics was not my best subject, Reed, but I don't think I'm fitting through there."

Like he didn't get an A in everything.

"Good eye," I replied. "I'll go. Meet me at the front door in thirty seconds."

Dash stared down at his watch. "I don't have a second hand."

"Just . . . count it," I told him.

Then I slipped through the window feet-first and landed with a bang on the metal desk below.

"Shhhhh!" I heard Dash hiss.

Alone in the darkened storage room, I rolled my eyes. Like there was anything I could do about the noise now. I hopped to the floor and navigated my way around the stacked desks and chairs. The frigid air in the basement was already freezing my sweat to my skin, and I shivered as I crept out the door. Once in the hallway, I raced up two sets of stairs to the front entry. Dash was already at the window, standing in full view under the security light. I opened the door as quietly as possible and let him in.

"I counted to forty-five," he said through his teeth.

"You're very literal. Anyone ever tell you that?" I asked.

He looked perturbed by the comment. "Let's just get this over with."

"Fine by me."

We took the stairs to Dean Marcus's office two at a time. In the upper hall, the faces of illustrious Easton graduates through the ages stared down at us disapprovingly from their ornate gilded frames. Their glares lent to the paranoid feeling that someone was going to step out of the shadows at any moment and read us our rights. Somehow, by the time we got to the outer door to the dean's office, I was clinging to Dash's arm. He didn't even seem to notice.

"Ready?" he said.

"Let's just hope Lewis-Hanneman didn't decide to work late," I joked.

All the color drained from Dash's face.

"I'm kidding!" I told him. It was past midnight, for goodness' sake. I reached out and opened the door.

The place was empty. We both breathed a sigh of relief. Dash crossed to the desk in two long strides and pulled out the leather chair. When he touched the mouse, the screen lit up.

"Nice. She doesn't power down. That saves us a couple of minutes," Dash said. He pulled out the keyboard tray and it smacked his knees. Automatically he reached around to adjust the chair and I jumped.

"Don't!"

Dash froze. "What?"

"She'll know someone was here," I told him.

Slowly, Dash grinned. "You're good."

"Thank you."

He pushed a bit further back and started to type. "Okay . . . e-mail system . . . password . . ." Quickly he keyed in something that involved a bunch of random characters and numbers. I think there was even a percent sign in there. He hit "enter." "Voilà. We're in."

I came around the desk. Sure enough, Dash was logged on to the Easton Academy e-mail system as Cara Lewis-Hanneman. The cursor blinked away, just waiting for us to type up a bogus message.

"How did you do that?" I asked.

"Lance Reagan," Dash said proudly. "Kid figured out the universal password his freshman year. He's gonna be the next Bill Gates. Okay. What's Blake's e-mail?"

I pulled a crumpled piece of paper out of my coat pocket and placed it on the pathologically neat desk. Unlike Dash, I didn't trust myself to memorize key information, even though my key information would have been a lot simpler to remember than his apparently was. This was just too important.

Dash typed in the address, then sat back. "Right. Now what do we say?"

Yeah. The hard part. How to do this without giving ourselves away.

"We have to keep it simple," I said. "If we try too hard to think like her, we'll screw it up."

"Right." Dash clicked on the subject line and typed in, *Meet me?* He looked up at me over his shoulder. "How's that?"

"Good, but get rid of the question mark," I said. "Makes it sound more urgent."

He deleted it without question. He moved to the message box and typed *Blake.*

"Wait. What if she doesn't call him Blake?" I said.

"What else would she call him?" he asked.

"I don't know? A nickname? Baby? Snookums? I have no idea," I replied. "But I know that I never put my brother's name in our e-mails. If I did, he'd know something was up."

"Okay. But what if she *always* puts his name in her e-mails? Won't not putting it there tip him off?" Dash said.

We stared at each other for a long moment. Outside the wind whistled and the windowpane behind the desk rattled in its frame.

"We're overthinking this," I said. "Just think urgency. She's worried. She needs to see him. Pretend you've been away from Noelle for a couple of weeks and you need to make her come to wherever you are."

Dash turned to the keyboard. Nothing happened. Not sure what that meant, but it had to mean something interesting.

"Here. Let me," I said.

Dash got up and I took his seat. I deleted the "Blake" and thought of Thomas. Of how the simplest words from him had made me long to be near him. I typed up the first words that came to mind.

I need to see you. Don't call, just come. Please. Friday night, 11 o'clock. The art cemetery.

I leaned back, satisfied. Dash hovered over my shoulder to read my masterpiece.

"That's it?" he said.

"That will do it," I replied confidently. "And I put in the 'don't call' so that he wouldn't try to get in touch before then. That could be bad."

"Brilliant," Dash said. "All right then."

He reached over my shoulder, moved the mouse, and clicked "send." My heart gave a lurch as the message disappeared from the desktop. The plan was in motion. There was no turning back now.

Then Dash opened up another screen. The "sent mail" screen. He quickly deleted the message we'd just sent from the folder.

"No evidence," he said.

"Wow. You're good too," I told him.

"Thank you," he said, preening.

I grabbed the paper with Blake's e-mail address on it and shoved it back into my coat pocket, then logged off the e-mail system. All bases now covered. I hoped.

"Just one question," I said, spinning the chair around to face Dash. "How is he going to get on campus with all the new security and the new rules?"

Dash stood up straight and lifted his shoulders. "He's Blake Pearson," he replied.

As if that answered everything.

DON'T CARE

Ariana's desk was not normal. I hadn't noticed it before, but now that I was sitting at it, attempting to study, I couldn't help making a few mental notes. One, it was completely devoid of memorabilia of any kind. There were no photographs, no ticket stubs, no party invitations or concert flyers, no pictures clipped out of *InStyle* magazine. The bulletin board was new and the only thing pinned to it was her class schedule, right smack in the middle. Near the corner was a cup full of natural wood pencils. A votive of fresh flower buds stood on the other corner. There was a stack of white, lined pads within reach and a light blue satin box with a lid. I could only imagine it contained paper clips or something equally innocuous. That was it. I glanced across the room at Noelle's desk, piled as it was with books, CDs, cosmetics, and small bags of all shapes and sizes, with eyeliners and pens and iPod and bottles of perfume sticking out of them. Photos both loose and in frames. Just tons of crap. It was a disaster area, but at least it was normal.

"How's the English lit coming, Reed?"

Ariana's voice sent a chill down my back. I looked over my shoulder at her. She sat on her flowered bedspread with her back against her throw pillow collection, her ankles crossed. On her lap was her history text and next to her was a notebook. Her pencil pressed into the page. She looked right through me, like she knew what I'd just been thinking.

"Fine," I said quickly.

"Good," she replied. Her lips formed a smile. Her eyes did not. I returned to my work.

"So, how many did you get on the guest list?" Noelle asked Kiran.

They were sitting on Noelle's unmade bed, books open but ignored. All they'd been talking about since we'd commenced our study session was their off-campus jaunt. Some club called Orchid in New York that only celebrities and debutantes could get into. The V.I.P. room. Five-hundred-dollar bottles of champagne. Limos waiting for them in town. They had it all set up. Too bad it was never going to work.

"Just twenty," Kiran replied. "We'll have to be very selective."

I tried not to shake my head at their total obliviousness. Did they really think they were going to sneak twenty people off campus right now? Had I not told them about the new security camera on the front gate, in full view of their little hole in the fence? Maybe they had the ability to become invisible. Another Billings Girl secret. When you reach junior year, you're given your superpowers.

"Believe me, I want to keep this small," Noelle told her. "The more selective the better."

"That's what I like to hear. So who are we including?" Kiran asked. Her thumbs were poised over her BlackBerry, ready to take down the pertinent information.

Noelle straightened her legs and flipped her hair over her shoulder. "*Not* Cheyenne. Let's start there."

"Fabulous decision."

"Girls. Let's not be rude," Ariana said in her stern voice.

"She's not going to come anyway," Kiran told her.

"All the more reason to extend the invitation," Ariana replied coolly. "It's always better not to burn bridges. You never know who Cheyenne might become."

"I already know. The frigid, cuckolded wife of some repressed gay senator," Noelle said. She and Kiran laughed, and Kiran dragged her hand across Noelle's.

"Charming," Ariana said.

Noelle rolled her eyes. "Fine. We'll invite her," she said. But when Ariana looked down again, Noelle shook her head at Kiran ever so slightly. Kiran smirked. Dissension in the ranks. Who knew?

"Okay, so, the four of us, *Cheyenne*," Kiran said, half-laughing. "Who else?"

"Uh, you guys can leave me out of it," I told them.

The room fell silent. I continued to pretend to read as if I hadn't just kiboshed the merriment.

"You're not serious," Noelle stated.

"I'm sorry. I'm just not in the mood to party right now," I told her without looking up.

I could feel them looking at one another.

"God, Reed, why don't you get over yourself already?" Kiran said.

My face stung. "Excuse me?" I blurted, turning to her.

"Sorry. I don't think I meant to say that out loud," Kiran told me, looking surprisingly chagrined.

Noelle shot her a look that could have wilted steel. "I think that what Kiran means to say is, you need to find a way to get past this," Noelle said. "And I think that this night is exactly what you need."

"Yeah, you've mentioned that," I replied. "I just don't agree."

"Look, Reed, I know things have sucked lately," Noelle said.

I snorted.

"Okay, that's an understatement, but I don't know what word would cover it, so just go with me on this, okay?" she said, pushing herself off her bed. "I know things have sucked, but that's exactly why we have to get out of here. This place has nothing but bad vibes lately. Don't you just want to get away from it for a few hours?"

"Of course I do," I told her. "But I can't do that until—"

"Until what? Until Josh is free?" Noelle said. "Even if he is found innocent, that could take months. What are you gonna do in the meantime? Just sit around here and wallow?"

"She's right. It's not good for your health," Ariana said, closing her book.

"Not to mention your complexion," Kiran put in.

I wanted out of this conversation. Especially in the next moment, when Noelle's eyes narrowed and took on that wicked sheen.

"Or maybe you just want to stay home so you can sneak out in the middle of the night again," she said.

Of course. Of course she knew I'd left the dorm the other night. Why did I ever think I could get away with it? Ariana and Kiran both looked surprised, however, so Noelle hadn't shared this information with them.

"When are you going to get it into your head, Reed?" Noelle said. "I—"

"Know everything. I know," I said tersely. "It's in my head already, believe me." I stood up, ignoring the ire on her face at being interrupted, and quickly gathered my things. "Let me ask you this. Do you know *where* I went?"

I didn't even know I was going to ask her that until the words were out of my mouth. But then I realized I had to know. Was she aware that Dash and I were sneaking around together in the middle of the night? Did she know why? Were we both in for some kind of retribution?

But as I watched, her defiant expression faltered slightly and I knew. She had no clue what I'd been doing. She was hoping I'd panic and tell her. So that she would be fully in the know, as she so loved to be.

"Guess not," I said, savoring that moment. That one moment

when I actually knew for sure that I knew more than Noelle. "In case you haven't heard, I haven't really been sleeping lately. Running calms me. So there you go. Now you've got all the facts. Enjoy."

I was already halfway across the room when she spoke again.

"You've been acting like a serious bitch lately," she said.

I paused with my hand on the doorknob. "What are you gonna do, Noelle? Kidnap me again? Force me to do some stupid errand? Kick me out of Billings?" I looked her dead in the eye and, even though I didn't fully believe it myself, part of me very much wanted to say it. So I did. "Do whatever you want. I really don't care anymore."

For once all three of them were stunned into silence.

Dash had never been to the art cemetery before. As I sat on the one divan, fiddling nervously with the key he'd lifted from Josh's room to get us in here, he strolled along the walls, admiring the rows and rows of artwork by the dim light of the one lamp we had dared to turn on. He'd risked everything sneaking into Josh's police-taped dorm to get this thing, and later he'd have to risk it again to sneak it back in so that the cops wouldn't notice it was missing. Yet there he was, his hands clasped behind his back as he strolled, like he was checking out a new SoHo gallery, instead of waiting for his dead best friend's brother to show up under false pretenses he'd concocted, after which he'd have to go back to his dorm and break the law. Again.

"What if he doesn't come?" I asked. My heart was pounding in my bones. My skull throbbed. My fingers were moist. I was a Ping-Pong ball of nerves.

He leaned in closer to an abstract painting, inspecting the signature. Infuriatingly composed. "He'll come."

"But what if he doesn't?" I clutched the key. Let it cut into my palm. "What do we do next?"

"Trust me. I know Blake Pearson." There was a slight laugh in his voice. "He'll come."

"How can you be so calm?" I asked finally.

"Meditative focus," he answered. "My older sister's kind of a New Age guru. Some of the stuff is actually useful."

"Your sister. A New Age guru," I said.

He turned to me and smiled. "Kind of the black sheep of the McCafferty clan."

"I can only imagine."

A door clicked out in the hallway. We both heard it. I got to my feet, my heart slamming against my rib cage. As the footsteps approached, I shoved my sweaty hands into the back pockets of my jeans and stood next to Dash. His size was comforting.

The door across the room opened. Blake Pearson stepped inside. He was different than I remembered him from Thomas's wake. He wore a casual sweater and coat and distressed jeans over hiking boots. His black hair was mussed and curled at the ends, which made his face look less thin. There was more color in his skin as well, but that could have been due to the extreme cold. He froze the moment he saw us, his blue eyes like ice picks. I looked up at Dash. Dash opened his mouth, and Blake turned to go.

Just like that. Without a word.

"Wait!" Dash shouted.

It was so loud I was sure the Easton security force was about to descend. But it had its desired effect. Blake stopped. Dash took the opportunity to cross the room and get between Blake and the door.

"We just want to talk to you, man," Dash said, raising his hands.

"Oh really?" Blake said. "About what?"

My heart shriveled and I had to gasp for air. His voice was exactly like Thomas's. I hadn't heard it in so many weeks, but I recognized it instantly. I backed up against the wall and blinked back the tears of shock. Pain.

"What's wrong with her?" Blake asked, with a dismissive glance.

"You all right?" Dash asked me.

I managed to nod. "I'm fine. Go . . . go ahead."

"You're sure." Dash was always the gentleman.

"I'm fine," I repeated firmly.

"All right. We know you were here that night, Blake," Dash said. "Why haven't you gone to the police and told them what you know?"

Blake crossed his arms over his chest. "All right, McCafferty, I'll bite," he said. "What do I know?"

"That Josh is innocent," Dash said, frustrated. "You and Hot Secretary are his alibi."

"Her name is Cara," Blake said, his eyes flashing with fury.

"Right. Sorry. Well, maybe you and Cara can do the right thing here," Dash said.

"The right thing? What are you, still living in black and white?" Blake said, pacing away. "If I go to the police, then everyone's gonna find out about me and Cara. She'll be fired, her husband will divorce her, and it'll be yet another scandal for Easton. As far as I'm concerned those are three very good reasons to keep my mouth firmly shut."

"No," I heard myself say.

"What?"

Blake truly looked at me for the first time. My knees felt like they weren't even there anymore, but somehow I pushed myself away from the wall.

"You have to tell," I said. "You have to. Josh's *life* is on the line here. I think that trumps your need to protect your mistress."

"Reed," Dash said.

"No. I'm right, aren't I? I mean, Josh could go to jail for the rest of his life and you're worried about your precious Cara's husband finding out that she's cheating? Well, news flash! She *is* cheating! Maybe she deserves to get a divorce!"

"That's it. I'm outta here," Blake said, gunning for the door.

"Don't you even want to know who really killed your own brother?" I blurted. My fingers curled into fists. Blake paused. For a moment I thought I'd actually gotten through to him.

Then he laughed. He tipped his head back and laughed. Loudly. Openly. Evilly.

"This is unbelievable!" he said. "Thomas is dead and he's *still* fucking up my life!"

Cannonball, this is my gut. Gut, meet the cannonball.

"What?" Dash blurted, his face contorted with disgust.

"Oh, come on, Dash, don't be so naïve! You know what life was like with Thomas around," Blake ranted, spittle appearing at the corners of his lips. "Him disappearing for days at a time. My parents getting woken up in the middle of the night by phone calls from some random police station in Miami or Vegas or freakin' Columbus, Ohio? Him showing up for events late, trashed out of his mind, making scenes, embarrassing my parents, embarrassing me!" He pounded his chest with both hands. I could feel the pain coming off of him in waves, the pent-up rage just bursting to come out. I knew what it felt like. Thomas had known what it felt like. Damn if the Pearsons didn't raise two very angry kids. "Thomas was a pointless waste of existence, and all he did was screw up the lives of everyone around him."

Blake paced around the small couch and sat down on the edge of it. Dash didn't move, but I could see his chest rising and falling, like he was trying to contain something huge. I hoped that meditation thing was as good as he believed it to be.

"Take this situation, for example," Blake continued, once he'd caught his breath. "Cara has refused to speak to me ever since the night of Josh's arrest. She's the love of my life and she won't even take a call from me. When I got that e-mail I thought . . ."

He trailed off and my heart broke for him. Just a touch. He clearly loved Ms. Lewis-Hanneman, as strange as that seemed to me. It was obvious by the torment in his eyes. And all we'd done here was give him false hope.

"Thomas is dead, and still he managed to fuck up the one good thing in my life," Blake said stoically. He stood up and turned to face me. "So to answer your question, no. I don't really care who killed him."

My stomach heaved. I had to swallow a dozen times to keep down whatever was trying to come up. There was pity on Blake's face before he turned to Dash again.

"Are we done here?" he said.

Dash said nothing. He'd gone catatonic. I knew the feeling. He didn't make any move to stop Blake as he slipped by him out the door. It wasn't until the outer door of Mitchell Hall slammed again that either one of us moved. I leaned back and slid down the wall until my butt hit the floor.

"What just happened?" I croaked, unable to blink or turn or do anything but stare straight ahead. Straight at the spot where Blake had stood just moments ago.

"I had no idea," Dash replied. "I always knew those two hated each other, but I thought it was just sibling-rivalry hate. Not real I-want-you-dead hate."

Dash sat down on the couch and hung his head in his hands. Our best hope to help Josh had just walked out the door and was probably already speeding south on Interstate 684.

"What do we do now?" I said.

Dash took a deep breath. "I have no idea."

KIND EAR

I hadn't spoken to Josh in nine days, and that was including him shouting to me across a crowded police station. Was he okay? Was he scared? Were they allowing his parents and his brothers and sisters to see him?

Was he thinking about me?

These questions occupied most of my brain space that Saturday night while I sat in front of the television in the parlor. Around me other Billings Girls studied, chatted, and laughed. Only a few, since most were upstairs getting ready for Noelle's off-campus romp. At least I had put to bed the question of whether or not I was going. The dirty-hair ponytail, ripped plaid pajama pants, and a Penn State sweatshirt had to be dead giveaways of my mood.

Part of me wished I could be up there with them. Wished I could be that carefree, thinking only about which shoes went with which dress and how to do my hair. I had just started to get into that stuff since meeting the Billings Girls and I missed it. I missed being able to enjoy those things. But I couldn't. Not now. Maybe not ever again.

"So, girls, which do you think is a better Christmas present for a new boyfriend with rock-star aspirations?" Cheyenne asked, bouncing into the room. She was wearing a red plaid skirt and a white ballet-neck top. Girl seemed to have an endless supply of season-appropriate outfits. "Backstage passes to the Fray and a meet-and-greet with the band, or three recording sessions in a state-of-the-art studio?"

"Recording sessions, definitely," Natasha replied, not looking up from her political science book. "The Fray doesn't fully qualify as 'rock,' anyway."

"Who the heck are the Fray?" Rose added.

Cheyenne blinked. "Both good points," she said, whipping out her gold-plated cell phone. "Studio time it is."

Unbelievable. Adam Robinson had had a birthday over the summer when we'd been dating, and I'd gotten him a Philadelphia Flyers hat. On sale.

Cheyenne quickly finished her business on the phone and sat down next to me. She smoothed her blond hair behind her shoulder and smiled in a friendly way.

"So, Reed. How are you doing?" she asked, lightly touching my shoulder before bringing her elbow up to rest on the back of the couch. "Have you heard anything from Josh?"

Natasha glanced up, probably as surprised as I was. Nobody had asked me this question. Nobody had asked me anything about

Josh's arrest or how it was affecting me. Until that very moment everyone, including Natasha, who was probably my best friend in Billings at this point, had chosen to take the don't-ask-don't-tell tack. I was touched that she'd thought to ask, but at the same time didn't remotely want to answer.

"No," I said. "I guess he's not allowed to make phone calls, really."

"You don't think he did it, do you?" she asked.

"I know he didn't."

"Good." She readjusted herself so that she was fully facing the TV and smoothed her skirt over her thighs. "The very idea that someone on this campus might have had something to do with it makes me wake up in a cold sweat some nights."

I couldn't imagine Cheyenne sweating, let alone admitting to it.

"Did you think that he *did* do it?" Natasha asked.

"No. I don't know," Cheyenne said. "I never knew either one of those guys very well, but Reed did. Does. Whatever. If she says he didn't do it, then I believe it."

She flashed her perfectly straight, whitening-stripped smile, and I felt inexplicably warm. In a good way.

"Now all we have to do is convince the rest of the world," I said.

"What I want to know is when they're going to figure it out," Cheyenne said. "I just hope this doesn't turn into one of those unsolved-mystery things, because that would not be pleasant."

I turned green at the thought and sank down lower in my seat.

"They'll figure it out," Natasha said confidently. "They're just missing some piece of the puzzle. As soon as they find it, it'll all fall into place."

We heard the sound of voices and footsteps descending the stairs. Apparently Noelle and her troupe were ready for their big night. Cheyenne cleared her throat and faced forward, her back to the door, as Noelle, Ariana, Kiran, Vienna, London, and a couple other girls gathered there. The moment I saw them, dressed to the nines in silk and diamonds, teetering on their high heels and made up like movie stars, I almost caved. This was fabulousness personified. Wasn't this the reason I'd wanted to be friends with them in the first place?

But I couldn't do it. There was a point to be made here. Plus there was too much risk. If I was caught where I wasn't supposed to be one more time, the dean would no longer be able to ignore it. Sneaking to the police station and to Hell Hall and the art cemetery was one thing—that was all for Josh. But this, this was just to get drunk and be seen. The only person I wanted to be seen by anymore was Josh Hollis. He was the only one who mattered.

"Well, we're off," Kiran said happily, lifting the slim strap on her red dress, which had fallen down over her shoulder.

"Have fun getting caught," Natasha said under her breath.

"Are you guys sure you want to do this?" I asked, turning in my seat. They really did look beautiful, standing there all in a row, all perfect skin and dramatic eyes and shimmering fabrics.

"Are you sure you don't?" Noelle asked. "Because we can wait a few minutes if you'd like to run off and take your first shower of the week."

There were a few snickers, which I ignored.

"You do realize that if you get caught, we're *all* going to be in trouble," Cheyenne said flatly.

"If we get caught, which we won't, nothing is going to happen," Noelle said, lifting her gold wristlet. "How long do you girls have to live in this dorm before you understand how it works?"

"I don't know," Cheyenne said. "With everything that's been going on lately, I'm not sure the old rules apply."

"Well, that's your problem then, isn't it?" Noelle said.

She walked over to the couch and leaned into it. "Reed, I'm not mad at you for last night, if that's what you're thinking. I know you're just stressed and overtired and you snapped. To be honest, I was actually kind of proud of you."

"She thinks she's rubbing off," Kiran put in.

I wasn't sure whether to feel sick or proud of that theory. I was more focused on how totally self-centered she was. Did she really think I wasn't coming to New York with them because I thought she was mad at me? Had she listened to absolutely nothing I'd said in the past week?

"So come on. Don't be lame. Come with us," Noelle said, nudging me with her bag.

"Thanks. I'd rather watch the Rudolph special for the two hundredth time," I told her.

Noelle's eyes darkened for a split second and my blood ran cold, but she quickly cleared it away with a smile. "All right then. You all stay here and work on spreading your asses. Meanwhile, we'll be hooking up and dodging paparazzi all night."

"Well, have fun. Try not to bring home any new diseases!" Natasha joked.

Noelle leveled her with a glare before turning and striding out. The moment the door closed behind them, we all laughed. Even me.

GROUNDED

It was only twenty minutes later that Mrs. Lattimer, our house-mother, scurried down the stairs, cinching the belt on her velvet robe tightly around her slim waist. Out of the corner of my eye, I saw her rush to the front door of Billings and I surreptitiously touched my toe to Natasha's arm. We both got up, intrigued, and Cheyenne and Rose followed. Mrs. Lattimer buttoned her night-gown all the way up until it was practically choking her, then opened the inner door. A blast of wind hit her in the face, and then in walked Noelle, Kiran, Ariana, London, Vienna, and the rest of them, followed by Scat himself, our neckless head of security.

"Girls! Whatever were you doing out at this time of night?" Mrs. Lattimer put on a good show of being shocked and appalled, but it was just that. A show. She knew every move Noelle made and was bribed big-time to keep her mouth shut about all of it.

Noelle glared at the woman. Then Dean Marcus walked in and closed the door behind him. An iron curtain of dread settled over all of us. I caught Natasha's eye. This was not good. Cheyenne was almost red with rage.

"In the parlor, please, everyone," the dean said. Only Vienna hopped to and rushed right into the room where we already stood. *"Now!"*

I'd never heard the dean yell before. Not really. Even Ariana flinched.

"Well. That was a waste of a good-hair day," Kiran said as she sauntered by me.

Noelle waited until everyone else was inside before taking her dear, sweet time strolling in behind them. She took a spot by the wall near the armchair where Kiran sat and struck a defiant pose. The dean looked around at all of us.

"I can't even begin to tell you how disappointed I am in you girls," he said sternly. "And not just those of you who flouted the rules tonight, but those of you who let them do it and didn't say a thing to stop them."

I felt Natasha tense next to me and I touched her arm. Now was not the time to debate the dean. We could do that later if we needed to, after he'd had a chance to calm down and maybe take a Tums. Or ten.

"You girls have the privilege of residing in one of the most prestigious dormitories on this campus. Billings was the first women's residence at this academy. Its alumnae have gone on to be some of the most powerful, well-respected women in the world. How do you think those women would feel about the way in which you have spat upon this institution with your actions?"

"They'd probably be pretty proud," Noelle said under her breath, but loud enough for everyone to hear. There were a few giggles and I just wanted to throttle someone.

"Ms. Lange, is there something about this situation that amuses you?" the dean asked, appalled. "Because if you like, we can go back to my office and you can tell me all about it before I expel you."

Someone gasped. But Noelle . . . Noelle just smiled, never taking her eyes off the dean. Cool as the other side of the pillow. "No, Dean. I'm not amused."

The dean hesitated a moment. Clearly he wasn't used to dealing with the likes of Noelle Lange. But he soon recovered and returned to his speech. Still, he didn't look in Noelle's direction again.

"I don't have to tell you girls that the rest of the school looks up to you. You set the example. When I appealed to the student body for their support, I was appealing primarily to you. They will follow whatever course you blaze, and you just blazed a course right into the woods and through a hole in a bloody fence!"

I thought the top of Cheyenne's head was going to blow right off. She was the type of girl who lived to set the right example, and she'd tried to do just that. But Noelle had ruined it for her. Noelle had turned lily-white Cheyenne Martin into a black sheep.

"Now, I warned you that there would be grave consequences for any indiscretions," the dean said. "Well, here they are."

No one in the room breathed. Every single girl around me tensed. Everyone except Ariana, who hadn't blinked since her return; Kiran, who just looked bored; and Noelle, whose defiant expression had not changed.

"From this moment on, when you are not in class, in the chapel for services, or in the cafeteria for meals, you will be in the library, seated at the center tables, studying."

"What?" Kiran finally snapped to and a few of the other girls stirred.

"Mrs. Lattimer will be there with you at all times to keep a head count," the dean continued, giving our housemother a stern look. As if, perhaps, she was being punished as well. She gripped the high collar on her nightgown and looked away.

"You can't do this," Ariana said.

"I believe I just did, Ms. Osgood," the dean said. "All of you, consider yourselves grounded for the remainder of the term."

He looked around the room, making eye contact with each and every one of us and just daring us to speak up again. No one did. Satisfied, he turned on his heel and stormed out, taking Scat with him.

The moment the door closed behind him, the room erupted in a hail of protests and whines. Noelle merely rolled her eyes and cut a straight line through the crowd, heading for the door. She was just about there when Cheyenne got right in front of her.

"I *told* you not to do this!" she ranted. "How could you be so selfish? Now you've gotten all of us grounded! I've never even been grounded by my parents!"

"There's a shocker," Kiran said.

Noelle stared down her nose at Cheyenne. She had a few inches on the girl and a much more imposing figure, but to Cheyenne's credit, she never backed up. Not even a step.

"Try to remember who you're dealing with, Martin," she said.

I expected Cheyenne to step aside. We all did. But she stood her ground. And in the end, it was Noelle who had to go around her to make her grand, sweeping exit.

DEVELOPMENT

"This one you are *not* going to believe!"

I awoke with a start and my history textbook slid off my lap and banged to the floor. Natasha stood in the doorway of our room, cell phone closed in her hand, her hair wild from the breeze on the roof. I brought my hand to my heart to make sure it wasn't on the outside of my body.

"Oh my gosh. I'm sorry. Did I wake you up?" Natasha said.

I looked around at the notebook on my bed, the clock, the mussed sheets. "Looks that way."

"I'm sorry. I didn't think you'd be asleep already," Natasha said. She sat down on the edge of my bed near my feet. "But you're never going to believe the dish Leanne just told me."

"Good news or bad news?" I asked, rubbing my temple with my fingertips. She looked pretty excited, so I was guessing it was good. Natasha didn't usually get her jollies from negative gossip. Not her style.

"I'm not sure. You tell me. Apparently, the gossip around the city is that Blake Pearson has disappeared."

"What?" All right, now I was awake. And on my feet. About a zillion thoughts flew through my head at once, none of them coherent. Something about guilt and death and anger and brothers. "When? I mean . . . how? Are you sure about this?"

"Well, it's not confirmed-confirmed, but in our circles these rumors are usually pretty accurate," Natasha said. The joy was gone, replaced by concern. "Why are you freaking out so bad?"

"Why am I freaking out so bad?" I blurted.

Because I just saw him. Because he left here so pissed off last night, he might have driven his BMW or whatever the hell he drove into a lamppost for all I knew. Because I had just met the guy for the first time, however convoluted and awful that meeting had been, and now he was gone.

"I'm sorry, that was a stupid question," Natasha said. "First Thomas and now Blake. Of course it's totally insane."

I stopped, a whole new line of thinking occurring to me. "Wait a minute. Do they think that somebody took him? That, like, whoever killed Thomas killed Blake now? Is that what they think?"

"It came up in the conversation," Natasha said, lifting her shoulders. "What if it's some kind of revenge thing? Like Mr. Pearson pissed somebody off somehow and now they're, I don't know, going after his kids. He's a pretty powerful guy in business, you know. Guys like that have equally powerful enemies."

"Sounds like you're writing a *Law & Order*," I told her.

"There's a reason why their plots are always 'ripped from the headlines,'" Natasha said, complete with air quotes. "When you think about it, it's kind of a good thing—in a sick, really twisted way. If someone did take Blake, then that kind of clears Josh, doesn't it? Since he's in police custody and all."

"Yeah. I guess it would."

I plopped down in my desk chair, trying to digest all this information. Trying to make sense of any of it. Maybe it was because I didn't grow up on the Upper East Side with all its alarm systems and bodyguards and whatever else they had, but I had a hard time believing that some pissed-off business associate of Mr. Pearson's was picking off his children. Of course, maybe that was the type of thing that happened all the time in the lives of the rich and famous.

Still, I couldn't shake the thought that Blake's disappearance was somehow related to the meeting with him last night. It was too coincidental. He'd just been here, just been confronted with the truth. And he'd been so angry. So venomously angry. It couldn't be a fluke. It had to mean something that he'd vanished so soon after he'd found out that his brother's best friend and girlfriend knew he'd been on campus the night of Thomas's murder. It had to mean something.

But what?

THE NEWS

"Who cares? It's just a couple of weeks and we were all going to be studying anyway. BFD," Noelle said the next morning, tearing off a piece of her bagel.

I stared across the cafeteria at the faculty tables. Ms. Lewis-Hanneman sat like a statue in front of her untouched food, staring at nothing. A few pieces of hair had fallen out of her usually perfect bun and she wasn't wearing any makeup. Her sweater was big and gray, the kind of thing you put on when you can't be bothered, or when you need some comfort. She'd heard the news. Obviously. My heart went out to her. I knew exactly how she was feeling. Knew all the horrible things that were going through her mind. How she felt like she might never be able to move again. At that moment, I didn't even care how awful she'd been to me in her office. I just felt for her.

Kiran sighed, looking down at the Sunday Style section of the *New York Times*. "Ever notice how much more appealing the outside world looks when you can't go there?"

"Kiran, Noelle is trying to apologize," Ariana scolded. She took a sip of her coffee and gazed over the cup at Kiran.

"I didn't hear an 'I'm sorry' in there," Natasha pointed out.

"She has her own way of apologizing," Ariana replied.

"Excuse me! I don't need anyone speaking for me, Ariana. Thanks," Noelle snapped. Ariana lifted her eyebrows and went back to her breakfast.

Over at the faculty table, Mrs. Naylor, the guidance director, greeted Ms. Lewis-Hanneman with a "Good morning." Ms. Lewis-Hanneman responded with a forced smile and nod, then went back to staring. She was so obviously desperate. I wondered if that was how I had looked when Thomas had gone missing.

But why didn't she try harder to cover it up? Wasn't her affair with Blake supposed to be a secret? I knew, God I knew, that it would be hard, but you'd think that she would at least try to act normal.

Cheyenne walked over with her tray of fruit salad and oatmeal and sat down at the far end of the next table, as always. Rose, London, and Vienna settled in around her. Apparently the Twin Cities had decided to defect back to their old locale. Noelle glared at them through narrowed eyes.

"Who the hell does Cheyenne think she is, anyway?" she said. "Her mother lives in Jersey, for God's sake. She's lucky she even got into Billings."

"We're all lucky we got into Billings," Ariana said lightly.

"What is with you today? You sound like my mother," Noelle said. "Even more so than usual."

Ariana simply lifted her shoulders and stifled a smile. She did seem oddly chipper.

"I don't know why you're all so mad at me anyway," Noelle continued. "I was just trying to help everyone have a little fun. Kiran set the whole thing up as much as I did. And you guys were all for it yesterday."

"Uh, we weren't," Natasha pointed out, lifting her fork.

"Thanks for the update, Ann Curry. It's duly noted," Noelle snapped. She tore another chunk off her bagel and popped it in her mouth. "Well, at least I know Reed's not mad at me."

I yanked my gaze away from Ms. Lewis-Hanneman and looked at Noelle.

"Ah! So you *are* in there," she said.

"I'm not mad at you?" I asked. Even though I wasn't, not really. I couldn't have cared less about groundings and thwarted outings just then. But I was curious as to why she thought so.

"Why would you be? You wanted to sit on your ass and do nothing, right?" Noelle said, her eyes sparkling. "Well, now you've got your wish!"

Just then the cafeteria door opened and Dash barreled in with Walt Whittaker at his heels. It had just started to snow when we arrived at the cafeteria, but now it must have been coming down. Their hair and shoulders were covered with snow, which Dash quickly brushed away, even as he made a beeline for our table. Walt, however, seemed content to let it melt and wet his hair.

"Did you hear?" Dash asked Noelle.

"Hear what?"

She leaned away from him, annoyed, as he pulled his scarf free and showered her with snow. Dash didn't notice. He was too busy looking at me.

"Blake Pearson," Dash said. "He disappeared."

I told him with my eyes that I already knew. Wished he could tell me with his what he was thinking. But his glance in my direction was fleeting. Good move, probably, if he didn't want his super-perceptive girlfriend asking questions.

"What? When?" Kiran asked.

Across the room, Ms. Lewis-Hanneman got up and grabbed her coat. I shoved my chair away from the table and quickly gathered my things as well.

"Ms. Brennan! Where do you think you're going?" Mrs. Lattimer demanded. She was sitting at a nearby table today in order to keep an eye on us.

"To the library, Mrs. Lattimer," I said as Ms. Lewis-Hanneman shoved through the far door. "I'm not hungry."

"Ms. Brennan!" Lattimer called after me.

Utterly pointless. I had to talk to Ms. Lewis-Hanneman. If Lattimer wanted to stop me, she'd have to send Scat after me.

THE TRUTH

Outside, the campus was blanketed in white. The gray sky swirled with snow, dusting the benches and pathways and giving everything that peaceful, silent glow. It was like a photo out of the Easton catalog. Exactly the kind of picturesque scene that had made me salivate to attend this school. How could I have ever known how little opportunity I would have to appreciate such things? Instead of strolling through the grounds with my new friends, laughing on my way to some intriguing class to broaden my mind, I was chasing down the secret girlfriend of my dead boyfriend's jerk brother. Put that in the catalog, Easton.

I shook my head and focused. There were more important things to do right now than dwell. Up ahead, Ms. Lewis-Hanneman speed-walked toward Hell Hall, her shoulders hunched, her hands tucked under her arms.

"Ms. Lewis-Hanneman!" I called out. She hesitated for a split second, then kept right on walking. "Wait up! Please?"

She ignored me. Nice try. I could run the forty in 5.75. I was by her side before she even made it to the steps.

"What do you want?" she asked. Her bare hand grasped the iron banister at the side of the stairs as she jogged up toward the door. Her fingers must have been like icicles. There were fresh tears on her face.

"I just wanted to see if you were okay," I said.

"Thank you for your concern, Miss Brennan, but I'm fine," she said flatly.

She yanked open the door to Hell Hall and I followed her into the lobby. The place was dark, quiet. Not much going on in these offices on a Sunday morning.

"Will you please stop following me?" Her voice was thick. She paused by the stairs to wipe under her eyes and bent slightly at the waist. I wanted to say something. Something to make her feel better. But I couldn't think of a word. "God, this is ridiculous. I can't stop crying," she said to the ceiling, not to me.

"It's okay."

"No. It's not. I don't cry in front of people," she said. "Especially not you."

She shot me a glare and I realized how young she was. Maybe not high school young, but younger than most of the other adults around here. And she could have been a Billings Girl with that glare.

"What's so bad about me?" I asked automatically.

"Do I really have to remind you that the last time we spoke you were trying to blackmail me?" she asked sarcastically. "You don't seriously think you're going to, what, comfort me now?"

She crossed over to a bench near the wall and dropped down. Tears streamed silently down her face as she tipped her head back and breathed deliberately though her nose, trying to regain control. Her fists clenched and unclenched as she breathed, but still the tears came.

"I'm sorry. I forgot," I said. "I didn't know this was going to happen and I . . . was desperate."

"Whatever." She sniffled and wiped under her eyes again.

"So . . . you don't have any idea where he is?" I asked.

"I'm not talking to you about this," she protested.

"Why not? You have to talk to someone," I said. "And I know exactly how you feel."

She scoffed. "Please."

I felt a white-hot surge of anger. How could she talk to me like that? Me of all people? "My boyfriend disappeared, too, remember?"

If possible, her face paled even further. I could only imagine she had no idea what to say. "I . . . that's right, I—"

"Forgot," I said. "I get it. Just don't talk to me like I don't know what's going on."

She stared at me for a long moment. I could see her reassessing me. Maybe respecting me.

"I just don't understand this," she said finally, shaking her head as fresh tears squeezed from the corners of her eyes. "Why is all this happening?"

I've asked myself that one ten billion times, lady.

"What do you think happened to him?" I asked.

"I have no idea," she replied, pressing her fingertips into her forehead and closing her eyes. "I've tried everything. His e-mails, all the numbers he's ever given me. It's all voice mail."

I took a deep breath. I knew I had to tell her. She had to know what I knew. Maybe it would help us figure this out. Maybe there was an answer in there somewhere. But I had a feeling it was not going to be pretty.

"I . . . um . . . I talked to him. To Blake," I said.

Her head snapped up. "You did? When? Where—?"

"It was before he went missing," I clarified.

She was on her feet again, practically trembling. "What did you say to him?" she asked, her eyes rimmed with red. She grasped the underside of my sleeves and held on. "Did you tell him the same thing you told me? Did you tell him you knew he was here that night?"

"Yeah, I did," I replied.

"Oh God." She buckled forward, like someone had kneed her in the gut, and sat down again. Her head hung between her knees and she rocked forward and back. "Oh God, oh God, oh God."

My throat was dry as sand. "What? What is it?"

She just kept shaking her head.

"Okay, you're scaring me," I said. "What is it?"

She looked up at me, pressing her hands into her thighs. The tears flowed freely as she continued to rock. I wondered if this was what a psychotic break looked like. "I swear I have no idea where he is."

"I've got that. What's the matter?" I asked.

"It's just . . . that night . . ."

My heart flipped up into my mouth as my knees lost all strength. I found myself, just like that, kneeling on the floor in front of her. My brain was so fogged through, I could barely see straight.

"What about that night?" I asked. "Ms. . . . *Cara*. What really happened that night?"

She took a deep breath through her nose, which was obviously clogged, and then it all came out with the air. "Josh walked in on us in the art cemetery. Blake got angry, of course. It was late. He thought we were safe. So he shouted at Josh. Asked him what the hell he was doing there so late. So Josh told him the truth. He said, 'Your stupid brother's on another one of his benders, so I had to come here to study.' He said it with a laugh, poor kid. Like he was making some joke we were all in on. But Blake, he . . . he—"

"He didn't think it was funny," I stated.

"No." She sniffed. "He basically lost it. He just shouted this stream of curses about Thomas and stormed out. He was so angry. . . ."

Oh my God. This was not happening.

"Where did he go?" I asked.

"I don't know," she whimpered, tears filling her eyes. "I stayed there and did some work for the Boosters' dinner, just hoping he'd come back. Josh stayed, too. I think he was worried about me being there alone. . . ."

That sounded like Josh. Ever the gentleman. Caring about everyone else. And now, because he'd cared about the wrong people that night, he was in jail.

"We left together a couple of hours later. Blake never came back," Ms. Lewis-Hanneman said, a tear spilling over. I could feel her just aching to confess. "The truth is . . . the truth is . . ."

"What?" I asked, trying to keep my voice from sounding strained. "What's the truth?"

She took a deep breath. Looked down at her hands. "The truth is, I have no idea where Blake was that night."

I sat back, my butt hitting the cold marble floor. Before me, Ms. Lewis-Hanneman quietly wept into her hands. All the pieces started to fall together in my mind. How angry Blake was at Thomas. How that anger had been festering all his life. How Josh's statement had clearly broken something inside of him. How he'd gone off in a rage. How there was no accounting for where he'd gone.

Blake had serious motive. And now, I knew, Blake had real opportunity. Josh had an alibi. A real, solid, alibi. Blake had none.

And now that he knew there were people who were aware he'd been on campus that night, he had disappeared. No one had taken him. He had fled. That much was now perfectly clear to me. These were not the actions of an innocent guy. He knew he was close to being caught and he'd gone on the run.

Blake had killed Thomas. Blake Pearson had murdered his own brother. And he'd been right in front of me just two days ago. He'd talked to me like I was sludge. I had let him go.

"You have to go to the police," I said quietly. "You have to."

"My life will be over," she said through her tears.

"No. No. I know one of the detectives," I told her. "He's a really good guy. Maybe you can talk to him, make some kind of deal to . . . I don't know . . . keep your name a secret or something. There must be some way to work it out."

She lifted her head. Her face was soaked, her eyes blurry and red. "But what if there's not? Without Blake, without my husband, without my job . . . I'll have nothing."

I got back to my knees and slid forward. I placed my hand on hers, just as Constance had so often done for me.

"I'm not saying he's guilty, Cara," I said. It was difficult, but I said it. "He may not be. There may be a perfectly good explanation for all of this. But we'll never find out unless you do the right thing."

She nodded and sniffled again, looking down.

"It's all gonna be okay," I told her, wishing I actually felt it.

"I'm sorry about Josh," she said to her hands. "He really is a good kid."

"You're the only one who can help him," I said.

"I know." She cleared her throat and took a deep breath. Then again, more firmly this time, "I know."

JINX

Thirty-four hours. That was how much time had passed since Cara Lewis-Hanneman had promised me she would go to the police. Thirty-four hours of waiting for the call. Of praying to hear Josh's voice again. Of aching with every inch of my body to tell someone what I knew. To clear his name.

But I didn't want to jinx it. More than anything, I wanted to see Josh again. And for some reason I felt that if I so much as uttered his name, Ms. Lewis-Hanneman would chicken out. She would vanish as well, and Josh's life would be over.

"Reed, will you please stop before you give me a seizure?" Noelle snapped, glaring down at my pencil.

I stopped tapping it against the library table, which I hadn't even known I was doing. "Sorry," I said automatically.

She blew out a huge sigh and lifted her thick brown hair over her shoulder. "Are you going to do some work, or can you only do that with Dash's help these days?"

I stared at her.

"He helped me with one thing," I said. "One project."

"And how did it turn out?" she asked.

I thought of Josh. Wondered if he was still in a cell somewhere or if he'd been freed. If maybe he was hugging his mom and dad right now, just waiting for the chance to call me. I glanced at my silent phone on the table next to me.

"Well, I think," I replied. "I guess I'll just have to wait and see."

The front door of the library slammed and everyone jumped. Within seconds, Walt Whittaker had rocketed into view at the end of the stacks that surrounded us, his skin ruddy from the cold and his breath short with exertion. My heart stopped beating entirely. I gripped my pencil with both hands. Mrs. Lattimer stood up and Whit leaned down to whisper something to her. Her face registered shock, then reset into its grim lines. She nodded. Whit turned to go.

Look at me, Whit! Look at me! Tell me what's going on!

But he didn't. He didn't so much as smile, wink, or frown in my direction. The big-boned bastard.

"All right, ladies," Mrs. Lattimer said. "It seems that the dean has called yet another emergency assembly."

A sizzle of intense curiosity and dread buzzed through our cozy group.

"What's going on?" someone whispered.

"God, not again," someone else moaned.

Noelle stood and gathered her things, as if this happened every day. Ariana slid her arms into her coat jacket and calmly picked up her books. I tried to hide my hopeful smile. After all, this could be anything. It wasn't necessarily what I wanted to be. Until I saw Josh with my own eyes, I was not going to allow myself to celebrate.

I felt Ariana's eyes on me and composed my mouth in a straight line. I could see, however, that she'd caught me. That she'd noted my almost-glee. She leveled me with one of her patented stares.

"What the hell is happening now?" Kiran asked the others.

"Good question," Ariana replied, never taking her eyes off me. "Let's go find out."

GOOD NEWS AND BAD NEWS

I hadn't been this excited to be inside the chapel since my first day at Easton.

"What's going on?" Constance asked me as we slid down toward the center aisle in our pews.

Josh has been cleared. He didn't do it. I told everyone he didn't do it and now, finally, everything is right again.

That was what I wanted to say, but instead I bit the inside of my cheek. I could not jinx this. Would not, for anything. If I said one word, Dean Marcus would walk out and tell us we were getting a new science lab, and I was not going to survive.

"I have no idea," I told her.

"You don't think there's been another murder, do you?" Diana Waters asked, pale as her crisp white shirt.

"I'm starting to feel like we go to Hogwarts," Lorna Gross grumbled.

"Oh, grow up, Lorna," Missy Thurber snapped. "You need new references."

I forced myself to face forward and clutched the low armrest at the end of the pew.

In ten minutes this would be over. In ten minutes we'd all know what this was all about.

The back door of the chapel finally closed and all the murmuring in the room came to an abrupt stop. Constance pulled her coat closer around her body and I wondered if it was chilly in the chapel. I felt as if my bones were portable heating rods, emanating warmth from the inside out.

Dean Marcus stepped up to the podium. For once there were no candles lit in the room, so the only light came from the weak fluorescents set high in the pointed ceiling. The effect on the dean was freakish. He looked like a corpse just risen from his grave. If I had been one to believe in omens, this would not have been a good one.

Oh God. He looked grim. This *was* an omen. He wasn't going to tell us Josh had been freed. He was going to tell us something awful.

And then, the door at the back of the stage area opened and Josh walked out behind the dean. My heart exploded. Seeing him was like every good thing that had ever happened to me happening again, all at once. Buying my first bike, scoring the winning goal against Lakeland last year, winning counties in lacrosse, getting into Easton. They all paled in comparison to this moment. I knew right then that I had never loved Thomas. There was no way I could have. Because nothing I had ever felt in his presence even approached what I felt at that moment.

I loved Josh. I loved Josh Hollis.

As everyone else in the chapel started talking again, gasping, questioning, hypothesizing, I imagined myself running down the aisle and throwing myself into his arms. I stared at Josh until he found me and smiled. For the first time in days, I felt free. Everything was okay. Everything was going to be fine.

Then two people walked out behind him. Two people who could only be his parents. His father, tall, with the same blond curls, but tamed and slicked to his temples. His mother, tall as well, but darker. Exotic-looking. Not at all what I would have imagined his mother to look like. They all sat in the front bench, once intended for the chapel choir. Josh's mother took his hand and clasped it.

I turned around and looked at Noelle and Ariana. Their shock made me smile even wider. But the longer I looked at them, the more I realized they weren't happy-shocked. They both looked as if they had swallowed something sour.

"Attention, students," the dean began. "Silence, please."

Somehow, everyone in the room managed to shut up. Probably because they were dying to hear what was going to happen next.

"It is my extreme pleasure to make the following announcement," Dean Marcus said. He looked anything but extremely pleased. He looked tired and pissed and about ready to retire. "Joshua Hollis has officially been cleared of any wrongdoing in the death of Thomas Pearson."

There was a huge roar. You'd think a gladiator had just slain a lion on the chapel floor. Happy tears filled my eyes. Constance hugged me and screamed. I laughed as everyone jumped to their feet and applauded and hollered. Josh went bright red and hung his head sheepishly. His father clapped along with the student body.

The dean attempted to bring order. "Silence, please!" He banged the podium a few times with the heel of one hand until everyone finally sat down again. For a long moment he eyed us grimly. "While I'm sure we can all agree that this is very good news, and not a surprise to any of us—"

Except Noelle. And Ariana. And Kiran. All of them had Josh convicted and sentenced a week ago.

"We all need to stick together now more than ever," the dean said. "I hate to remind you of this terrible fact, but this means there is still a killer out there somewhere."

Any remaining whispers and murmurs died. Even I stopped smiling.

"So while I expect all of you to welcome Josh back with open arms, I must remind you to exercise caution on campus and off, report anything suspicious, and please, just . . . take care of one another."

From several pews away, Josh and I stared into each other's eyes. I was never letting him out of my sight again. Never.

REUNION

Somehow, Josh and his parents ended up by the exit door, accepting congratulations and well-wishes from anyone who cared to give them on their way out. It was like a receiving line at a wedding. I had only been to one in my life, when my cousin Shelby married that slimeball Emmit, and that receiving line had ended in a fistfight between the groom and his best man, but this one was much more peaceful. Everyone seemed genuinely happy to see Josh again. Even Noelle and Ariana stopped by to say hello. Kiran, I noticed, did not. She hid in a group of freshmen who were probably too nervous to stop, and used them as camouflage to get out the door.

I hung back and waited. Waited until the very last person had left the room and only the Hollis family and the dean remained. I had no idea how Josh was going to treat me in front of his parents, so I was feeling quaky and nervous as I approached. Imagine my relieved surprise when he turned around and hugged me right off the ground.

"Oh God, it is so good to see you," he said.

He squeezed me and out came a few tears. I wiped them quickly away as he replaced me on the ground. He smelled like Ivory soap and freshly cleaned laundry. I wanted to press my face into his chest and just breathe, but his parents were hovering. Hovering with smiles on.

"Mom, Dad, this is Reed Brennan," Josh said, keeping one arm around my waist. "These are Susan and Alan Hollis."

"Nice to meet you," I said, sniffling.

Mrs. Hollis smiled and shook my hand. "It's a pleasure to meet you, Reed. Josh hasn't stopped talking about you since maybe the second week of school."

I looked at him, surprised, and he blushed. I hadn't even known him the second week of school. Not really.

"I hear we owe you a debt," his father said kindly. His hand was large and warm around mine. "You convinced that woman to come in and tell the truth."

"Thanks," I said, unsure how to respond.

"Mr. and Mrs. Hollis . . . Josh," the dean said quietly. "If we could all go back to my office for a bit. There are just some details we need to iron out."

"Of course," Josh's father said, his voice booming. "But I think we can let the kids have a couple of minutes alone, can't we, David? After all, they haven't seen each other in days."

There was a twinkle in his eye as he said this. The dean looked like he'd rather deep-sea dive with sharks than oblige.

"Fine. Five minutes," he said. "Then you can join us in my office, Joshua."

"I hope we'll see you again, soon, Reed," Josh's mother said, touching my arm.

"I hope so too," I replied.

Then they were gone. The door was closed. We were alone. Josh pulled me to him, placed his hands on either side of my face, and kissed me so deeply I forgot where I was. I fell into him, clutching at the sleeves of his sweater as another happy tear slid across my cheek.

"Your father's cool," I said, half out of it.

Josh laughed and the sound filled the chapel. It was so good to hear his laugh. "That's not something you want to hear after you kiss a girl."

"You know what I mean. Giving us a chance to talk," I said, pushing him.

"Who said anything about talking?"

Josh kissed me again. I wished we could stay like this forever. And ever and ever and ever. When he finally let me go again, I had to sit down. I dropped into the last pew and he sat next to me, nudging me down with his hip. His hand found mine and clasped it. Neither one of us wanted to stop touching each other, even for a second.

"Why didn't you ever tell me you saw Blake here that night?" I asked.

Maybe it wasn't the most romantic thing to say, but I'd been dying to ask him that for days. Josh blew out a sigh and I knew he'd been thinking about this a lot. Of course he had been. He'd had plenty of time to ponder the fact that if he'd said something earlier, he might never have been in jail.

"I never really thought about it," he said. "After Thomas died, everything sort of blurred together anyway. And believe me, I never thought I was going to need an alibi."

"Did you hear about him? About Blake?" I asked.

Josh nodded grimly. "No one's heard anything?"

"Not that I know of. But did you know he disappeared right after Dash and I confronted him?" I asked.

"What?"

"He found out that we knew he was here that night and he vanished," I told him. "Kind of a big coincidence, don't you think?"

Josh turned slightly so that his knees touched mine. I ignored the thrill that went through me. Every touch was about a zillion times more intense today.

"You don't think . . . do you think Blake did this?" he asked.

"I don't know, but it *is* suspicious, isn't it?" I said.

Josh looked like he was about to throw up. He sat back again and slumped, taking a long, deep breath.

"Are you all right?" I asked, my heart thudding.

"It's just a lot, you know? I've known these guys my whole life. Blake can be a dick, yeah, but I can't imagine him . . . with my baseball bat. . . . But I guess he could have gotten it, right? He could have gone to our room and gotten Thomas to come with him and taken the bat. . . ."

He squeezed his eyes shut and tipped forward, releasing my hand for the first time so that he could grasp the back of the pew in front of us.

"I'm sorry," I said, putting my hand on his back. "I shouldn't have brought it up. I just thought you'd want to know what was going on. . . ."

"No, it's okay," Josh said, taking a few heaving breaths. "It's fine. I'm fine."

After a couple of minutes he sat up again. His face looked waxy and pale, but he was otherwise okay. He gave me an apologetic glance, then laced his fingers through mine again.

"Let's just not talk about this anymore, okay?" he suggested, trying to smile. "As far as I'm concerned, this is the police's problem now. Not ours. From now on, we just . . . move on. Get back to normal. Is that okay with you?"

I smiled and leaned in for a quick kiss. "Okay?" I said. "It sounds perfect."

REGRET

"So now they want to bring Blake Pearson in for questioning," Noelle said, lowering her copy of the *New York Times*. Everyone on campus had one. Or a copy of the *Post* or the *Hartford Courant*. The new developments in Thomas's case had made the front page all up and down the East Coast, apparently. "That boy always was a little too intense for my taste."

I looked at Josh across the wide cafeteria table. He had been back at school for two days and was looking more and more like himself each day. This morning he wore a tan sweater with a hole near the collar and a paint stain on the sleeve. He'd already devoured a chocolate doughnut and was on to a cinnamon. Our legs were hooked together at the ankle under the table. He shook his head slightly at Noelle's comment and continued to eat.

"Please. You had a major crush on him," Kiran said as she texted on her BlackBerry.

"Kiran!" Noelle blurted.

"You did?" Dash asked, nonplussed. "When was this?"

Kiran went green, but continued to type away with her thumbs.

"I never had a crush on Blake Pearson," Noelle said huffily. "Maybe I thought he was cute for five seconds in eighth grade, but then he went through that awful awkward phase," she said with a shudder.

"Right. Pizza-Face Pearson," Gage said, laughing with his mouth full. "Extra pepperoni!"

"You're one to laugh, Coolidge, considering your awkward phase never ended," Natasha said.

Gage's mouth snapped shut. Thank God. I really didn't need to look at his half-chewed food any longer.

"It must have been so difficult for him, with Thomas for a younger brother," Ariana mused. "He never had an awkward phase, did he?"

"No, but he did have a jackass phase," Kiran said.

"Kiran!" Ariana scolded. "You're not supposed to speak ill of the dead."

Kiran looked up and pulled a stupid-me face in my direction, then set her BlackBerry aside. "Sorry. I'm texting Tiara in Milan. I have no filter with her."

"Ah, TyTy." Noelle sighed as she speared a grape with her fork. "I miss that girl and her total inability to edit herself. When is she coming back to school?"

"Oh, never. She just landed *Vogue*." Kiran's jealousy was plain to the world.

I stared at Kiran blankly. I had no idea who Tiara was, nor did I care, but she took my lack of expression to be my usual fashion-world ignorance.

"The cover," Kiran explained. "You don't go back to being a mere human after that."

"Oh," I said.

"Maybe Tiara knows where Blake is," Noelle said with a knowing smile. "Those two always seemed to find each other whenever there was no one else to find."

"She found Thomas a few times too," Gage put in.

"God, it's a wonder those two didn't kill each other sooner," Noelle joked.

"Noelle! What the hell is wrong with you?" Dash said, dropping his fork with a clatter.

Noelle lifted her hand to her chest. "Sorry. God. Have a coronary. It was just a joke."

"Can we please talk about something else?" Josh blurted.

Everyone fell silent. Noelle took a deep breath and moved her utensils to the sides of her plate, lining them up carefully before she finally spoke.

"I'd think you'd be happy the focus has shifted to Blake, Josh," she said. "After all, that's what got you out of jail, didn't it?"

Josh said nothing. I could see the blood working its way up his neck and into his face.

"Noelle, drop it," Dash said.

"All I'm saying is, it's good to finally have a suspect that makes perfect sense," she said with a shrug. "Those two always hated each other. We all saw it."

Josh looked like he was about to explode. If he did, I knew it would not be pretty and that it might be quite loud. Something for everyone in the cafeteria to hear. My protective side kicked in.

"Why is it that every person the cops suspect makes perfect sense to you until they're cleared?" I asked Noelle.

I could feel the implied "ooooooh" from everyone at the table. Kiran pushed back as if she was avoiding the line of fire and Dash shot me a pitying look. But I wasn't about to back down.

"What do you mean, Reed?" Noelle asked icily.

"She's right," Josh said. "First Rick DeLea, now Blake. I heard you even had me drawn and quartered for a few days there, Noelle. What the hell is up with that?"

Noelle glared at Josh before her eyes slid slowly to me. As if I had told Josh how very guilty Noelle thought he was. But I hadn't. If I had to guess, my money was on Gage. But good luck making Noelle believe that.

I had a feeling that Noelle was starting to regret ever inviting me to live in Billings.

AN IDEA

Normal. We'd been trying to find it all semester. Now, with everyone safely back inside Easton's gates, we settled into some semblance of it. Everyone was busy studying. The library, still the Billings Girls' home away from home, was now jam-packed with students from every class holding cram sessions and project meetings. Even I was able to absorb information again, which was a very good thing, since I had so much to catch up on. I found that Dean Marcus's grounding turned out to be a blessing. Since I spent every waking hour outside of class in the library, studying was about all I could do.

There were still a few clues here and there that not all was right in the world of Easton. Especially for me. Every now and then I would see someone out of the corner of my eye and think it was Thomas. My heart would catch and I would turn, and the guy in question would actually look nothing like him. It was just my brain playing tricks on my already battered heart, and I'd have to remember all over again that Thomas was dead. Even though I was with

Josh now, it hurt every time. To know that he was gone forever. That I'd never see that smile again. It still hurt.

Meanwhile, Josh refused to be anywhere within a five-foot radius of Noelle. Since I had to sit at the same table with her at all times, it made seeing him difficult, but we found our ways. Timing our bathroom breaks so that we'd be coming out at the same moment, walking from classroom to classroom together, sitting at the far end of our table at mealtimes, ignoring the conversation around us. Still, the chill between them was palpable, and Noelle hadn't said all that much to me either since our showdown in the cafeteria. I hoped she wasn't using that time to plot against me. I was not in the mood for more hazing.

Also, there were the headlines. Each day they grew more and more scathing. Easton Academy was dragged through the muck every which way possible. The school was derided for turning out murderers and drug dealers in one article, yet taken to task for installing security cameras in the next—as if the board didn't have the right or the cause. The student body started to develop a palpable anger. There were details in one article that could only have been related by someone who attended the school. Whether it was an alumnus or one of the kids who had been pulled out after Thomas's death, no one knew. But no one wanted to believe it was someone who was still on campus. In our delicate state of being, that kind of betrayal would have been too much for anyone to take.

I tried to ignore all of it. Josh was safe, and I had to keep my grades up if I wanted to come back to Easton in the spring. Of course I still wanted to see Thomas's murderer brought to justice, but my role in that particular drama was over. As Detective Hauer had suggested in the beginning, I decided to let the police do their job, and I would do mine: pass finals.

That's exactly what I was trying to do late one Tuesday night in the library. I was so engrossed in my chemistry flash cards that I didn't even notice when Dean Marcus walked in.

"What's he doing now? Checking up on us?" Noelle grumbled from across the table and a couple seats down.

"I feel bad for him," Cheyenne said. "Look. He's aged at least ten years since the beginning of the term. I bet he wishes Headmaster Cox had never retired."

"Who's Headmaster Cox?" I asked.

Everyone looked at me like I'd just asked how to add two and two.

"Headmaster Cox ran this place for thirty years," Ariana told me. "He retired last semester. Dean Marcus is technically the dean of students. He's only acting as head of the academy until they can find a new headmaster."

"How did you not know that? Everyone knows that," Kiran said.

"She's new, remember?" Cheyenne defended me.

I glanced up then and found Dean Marcus talking with Mrs. Lattimer way down at the far end of our sequestered area. He looked frail, like he hadn't eaten in days, and he was obviously graying. Cheyenne was right. This school year had taken a big toll on the man. What an awful year to be acting as interim headmaster.

"Maybe he should quit," Noelle said. "Spare us all the misery."

"Noelle!" Cheyenne was shocked. "Dean Marcus *is* Easton. I couldn't even imagine this place without him."

"I could," Noelle said. "Gladly."

"You don't mean that," Cheyenne protested, shaking her blond hair back.

"Yes. I do. The guy's an asshole, Cheyenne," Noelle said. "He *grounded* us. Us! This weekend is the last weekend before finals and we can't even leave this library, let alone campus. I mean, who does he think he is?"

"He's the dean of students and he's worked here since he was a professor. He cares about this place and its reputation," Cheyenne replied flatly. I saw something register in her eyes. An idea. "In fact . . . we may be able to use that to our advantage."

"What do you mean?" I asked, intrigued.

"I think I just came up with a way to get us off campus after all."

"*You* have a plan," Noelle said doubtfully.

"Yes." Cheyenne grinned, sitting up straight. "Yes. In fact, I do."

She placed her hands on the table and stood, then smoothed the front of her white sweater and patted her hair. My skin prickled with curiosity. She turned and strode right over to Dean Marcus and Mrs. Lattimer, all confidence and smiles.

"What's she up to?" Kiran asked, pulling her earbuds from her ears.

Noelle sighed and returned to her work. "I could not care less."

A DEAL

"Did my gown come in?" Natasha asked, clutching her cell phone to her ear as we walked back from the library later that night. It was a beautiful crisp night with thousands of stars blanketing the sky. I kept my head tipped back as we walked; for the first time in weeks, I was able to focus on the beauty of the world. "How does it look? Okay. Yes. We'll have the last fitting the day before Christmas Eve. No, I'll do it. I'll call him, Mom. You have other things to worry about. Okay. Love you too."

She hung up the phone, smiling.

"Aw! Miss Moral Center loves her mommy! How sweet," Noelle teased.

Natasha rolled her eyes but said nothing.

"What's the gown for? You 'coming out' to society?" Kiran asked, cackling.

"Kiran," Ariana scolded, "that is so inappropriate."

"No. It's hilarious. Really," Natasha said flatly, patting Kiran's shoulder. "And they say models have no brains."

Kiran scoffed but could not, in fact, come up with a comeback. Which clearly pissed her off.

"No, the gown is for the embassy ball on Christmas Eve," Natasha said. "I go every year."

"The embassy ball?" I asked. My vision fogged over for a second as I snapped my head forward. Reverse head-rush.

"My mother is the ambassador to the United States from Zimbabwe," Natasha said. "She holds this ball in D.C. every year."

I almost tripped on my own feet. "Your mother's an ambassador? You never told me that."

Natasha shrugged. "Never came up."

I felt stung. I thought Natasha and I had grown close, but this was a huge thing she'd never deigned to share with me. "I can't believe you never told me."

"I don't know what *your* mother does," Natasha pointed out.

Oh. Right. And you never will.

"What *does* your mother do?" Kiran asked, tilting her head toward me.

"Nothing interesting," I replied, wishing like hell I'd kept my mouth shut.

"No, come on, Reed. Tell us," Noelle teased. "I'll bet she drives a bus. No! She works in a mill."

I felt like I was going to burst into embarrassed tears at any second. Noelle was just goading me. She knew all about my family— or so she'd implied on several occasions. She'd probably read my file at some point, considering she seemed to have access to anything she wanted. I wondered if she knew only that my mother was on disability, or if she also somehow knew that all my mother ever did anymore was pop pills and make everyone's lives miserable— for the few hours a day she was awake.

Up ahead the windows of Billings glowed with welcoming light. If I could just deflect this until we got inside . . .

"Do people really still *do* that?" Kiran asked.

"You may as well just tell them, Reed. I'm sure it's nothing to be ashamed of," Ariana said.

At that moment the front door of Billings opened and Cheyenne popped her head out. "Hurry it up, girls! We're all meeting in the parlor."

Noelle paused. I knew all thoughts of my family's occupations were forgotten. I'd been saved by mini-Martha. "Oh, this girl has gone too far. She's calling meetings now?"

Cheyenne had disappeared from the library with Dean Marcus about an hour earlier. Apparently whatever they had talked about had gone Cheyenne's way, because she was grinning from ear to ear as she held the door open for us and ushered us in. We all dropped our coats and bags in the foyer, where a fire crackled and the Christmas tree twinkled, and followed her to the parlor. The rest of the dorm had already gathered. Mrs. Lattimer stood by the doorway, her expression pinched, her hand at the collar of her shirt.

"Have a seat, have a seat," Cheyenne said to us, like she was the hostess and we were the guests. Noelle ignored her and stood behind the couch. Natasha dropped onto an ottoman, but Ariana, Kiran, and I stayed standing. As annoyed as I was at Noelle, it felt like the type of moment for choosing sides, and my instinct was still to stay on hers.

Cheyenne stepped over Vienna's outstretched legs and faced us at the front of the room. She was practically oozing with self-satisfaction.

"I have exciting news," she said. "The dean and I have made a deal. Trey Prescott and I have agreed to do an exclusive interview with the *New York Times*, all about how amazing it is to be a student at Easton, and in return . . . he's going to let us off campus this weekend!"

There were excited gasps all throughout the room. Noelle's hand tightened around the ornate wooden frame of the couch.

"Orchid V.I.P. room, here we come!" Vienna shouted, throwing up her hands.

I thought Noelle might rend the furniture in two. I imagined all the girls sitting on the couch falling on their toned butts on the antique rug.

"Actually, we're not going to New York," Cheyenne said, quieting everyone again. "The deal stipulated that we go to a prearranged spot. So we're going to my family's summer house in Litchfield."

Noelle's grip instantly relaxed. She snorted a laugh. "Wow. How fabulous," she said. "Next you're going to tell us your dad and stepmom are going to be there to chaperone."

Cheyenne glanced at Mrs. Lattimer. She nodded shrewdly, cleared her throat, and left the room. Noelle watched the woman go with her mouth slightly open. Someone other than her had just gotten Lattimer to leave us alone. Cheyenne was pink with pleasure.

"Actually, the dean did call my father and asked him to chaperone. Which, of course, Daddy said he would do."

Everyone groaned. Cheyenne held up a hand.

"But Dad just called me five minutes ago and told me he can't actually make it," she added. "He trusts me. Trusts us. So we're on our own."

"And he'll cover for us?" Rose asked.

"Of course he will," Cheyenne said. Just like that, she'd won the crowd over again. Cheyenne looked right at Noelle as everyone else squealed with delight. "So it looks like we'll be having our yearly off-campus party after all!"

There was a round of cheers and the meeting started to break up. All around me, girls were planning what to wear, which guys to invite, how drunk they wanted to get. All the while, Cheyenne and Noelle continued to glare at one another. Noelle looked murderous.

Cheyenne was the first to break eye contact. She walked around the couch and approached us.

"Nice work," Noelle said, crossing her arms over her chest. "You got the dean to agree to let us go hang out in Hicksville. What're we going to do? Go cow-tipping? Take a historical hayride through the square?"

Cheyenne smiled and shook her head. "At least I got him to let us off campus, which was something you couldn't do. Oh, no, wait—something you didn't even *try* to do."

Noelle stared down her nose at Cheyenne, silently fuming. "Well, maybe I'm just not a natural kiss-ass."

"You can't just intimidate your way through life, Noelle. That's not how it works," Cheyenne said calmly. "Sometimes you have to work *with* people. Speaking of which, Reed, I have a favor to ask."

She shifted her attention to me before Noelle could formulate another comeback.

"A favor?"

"Yes. The dean thought it might be a good idea to have at least one scholarship student in on the interview. You know, to show the world that we're not just a bunch of overprivileged snobs," she said with a small laugh. "Of course, I immediately thought of you."

"Oh, I—"

There was literally nothing I wanted to do less than have some reporter grill me on my months at Easton. Did I actually have anything good to say?

"You won't have to talk about Thomas and all that drama unless you want to," Cheyenne said, correctly guessing the source of my hesitation. "You can focus on the teachers, the classes, the dorms. Tell them what a world-class education you're getting. I think the dean would really appreciate it."

My gut twisted in twenty different ways, but I got her point. "Okay," I said. "If it'll help him ease up on us, then sure. I'm in."

"That's great!" Cheyenne said gleefully. Then, much to my

surprise, she grabbed me in a quick hug. "I'll let you know as soon as I have all the details. Have a good night, girls!" she trilled. Then she bounded out of the room like a happy puppy.

I didn't dare look anyone else in the eye. I simply turned around, grabbed my stuff, and followed.

BUDDY-BUDDY

I was just dozing off that night—something I was pleasantly surprised I could still do after all those sleepless nights—when the
door to my room opened, spilling dim light in from the hallway. I
sat up straight in my bed and my heart caught when I saw Noelle's
shadow entering the room. Ariana and Kiran were right behind her.
Here it was. My new round of hazing. Well, this time I wasn't going
anywhere without a real fight.

"What the hell are you guys doing?" Natasha asked before I had
the chance.

Ariana flicked on the lights. She wore a white nightgown with
lace at the wide neck and carried a Burberry shopping bag. Kiran, in
a red nightie, placed a martini shaker and a bottle of vodka down on
my desk. Noelle, wearing a black silk pajama set, added four martini glasses. I was officially confused. They were all in PJs, so they
weren't dragging me anywhere, and apparently they were setting up
a bar.

"I couldn't sleep, so I went to Kiran's," Noelle explained. "Kiran thought a couple of drinks might help, but I never drink alone." She picked up the shaker and started shaking. "So here we are."

Natasha and I looked at one another across the room. We could throw them out, but that might cause more trouble than it was worth. If we let them stay and have one drink, they'd go faster and happier. We communicated all of this silently; then, decision made, Natasha threw her covers aside with a huff and we joined them at the desk.

"Make mine a double," Kiran said.

Noelle expertly poured out a glassful of liquid. Ariana took a jar of olives out of her bag and speared two with a toothpick.

"We should open a bar when we get out of here," Noelle joked to Ariana.

"I think we would do very well," Ariana replied.

I stared at them. They were in too good of a mood. Where exactly was this going?

"Reed?" Noelle asked as Kiran took her drink and perched on Natasha's desk chair.

"None for me, thanks," I said.

"Oh! Is living with Miss Moral Center rubbing off on you?" Noelle asked.

"No, it's just I can't be hungover tomorrow. I have class and a lot of work," I said.

"You're having a drink," Noelle told me, holding a half-full glass out.

My heart thumped. "No. I'm not."

"You're having a drink," she said. "You can either drink it, or I can dump it on your head. Your call."

My teeth clenched together. I could have killed the person who decided that having no locks on our dorm room doors was a good idea. Of course, a lock wouldn't have stopped Noelle anyway, I knew. She found a way around everything.

"Fine."

I took the glass from her and sat down on my bed with no intention of drinking it. Noelle smiled her triumph, then poured out drinks for Natasha, Ariana, and herself. Soon we were all seated around the room, sipping. Or pretending to sip, as it were.

"So . . . ," Natasha said finally.

"So what?" Noelle asked.

"So what are you doing here?" I asked.

"Can't friends share a midnight drink with friends anymore?" Noelle asked.

"We just came to talk," Ariana clarified. "The term is almost over, and lately we haven't really had time to bond."

"Bond." Kiran hiccupped a laugh. "I love that word."

Clearly she had been drinking way before Noelle had showed up at her room. "Plus we figured it would be nice to have a little fun," Noelle said, lifting her glass. "Since we won't be having any this weekend."

"Oh, so that's what this is about. You want to bash Cheyenne," Natasha said, leaning forward.

"Who needs to bash her?" Noelle asked innocently. "Everyone already knows that her idea of fun is totally lame."

"The rest of the dorm seemed to like it," I pointed out.

"The rest of the dorm is too stupid to realize how boring it's going to be," Kiran said.

"So you guys aren't going to go?" I asked.

"Of course we're going to go," Noelle said. "If only to rub her nose in her incredible failure."

They all laughed and clinked glasses.

"I think you're just annoyed because she's managed to do what you couldn't," Natasha said to Noelle. "I think it kills you."

"Anyone can suck up to authority, Crenshaw. I prefer to do things my way," Noelle snapped.

"Unfortunately, your way got us grounded," Natasha said under her breath.

"Oh, like you had so many better things to do," Noelle said. "Last time I checked, your entire social life had been unceremoniously drop-kicked out of this school, never to show her pore-clogged face again."

Natasha looked as if she'd been slapped. Not only had Noelle just insulted Natasha's girlfriend, but she was throwing around Leanne's expulsion, when we all knew very well that Noelle was the one who'd gotten her expelled.

"But let's not talk about the past," Noelle said, turning to me. "I want to talk about Miss Reed."

Oh God. Here we go.

"You seem very buddy-buddy with the automaton," she said.

"Excuse me?"

"Cheyenne. She's talking about Cheyenne," Ariana said firmly.

"Yes, her. The dean's robot. What's that all about?" Noelle asked.

"I'm not buddy-buddy with her," I replied. "She just asked me to do the interview."

"Right. The interview. That which she used to go over my head and make plans without me. Without any of us," Noelle said.

"Look, I'm just trying to help us all out," I said. "The dean's pissed at us, and if this helps him be less pissed, then I'm going to do it. I don't love Cheyenne, but I think it was smart of her to offer an olive branch. After everything that's happened, we need a little good PR."

Noelle stared at me. For a moment I actually thought she was seeing the validity of my point. But then she scoffed. She lifted the toothpick from her glass, brought her teeth down on the olive, and pulled it off.

"She's got you all totally brainwashed," Noelle said, shaking her head like it was just too funny. "It's almost pathetic, really. I so hate to see my friends all brainwashed."

Unless, of course, it was by her own hand.

"And that's why she needs to be taken down a peg."

A heavy sense of foreboding settled over the room.

"What do you mean, exactly?" Ariana asked, intrigued.

Noelle shrugged and smiled. "I have my ways."

"We know you do," Kiran said, half-gleeful, half-resigned.

And suddenly I felt sorry for Cheyenne. Because when Noelle decided to knock someone down a peg, that person usually ended up getting knocked all the way down to the pits of hell.

THE FUGITIVE

It was stifling in the dean's office. For some reason he had a fire lit in the old fireplace—maybe to give the photos a cozier and quainter feel—but it was making my very blood boil. I'd already shed my sweater and now sat in the center of the room between Cheyenne and Trey wearing a Philadelphia Eagles T-shirt that I was seriously regretting wearing. It made me look like the scholarship student I was. It made me feel like anything but a Billings Girl. And if I was going to survive what had turned into nothing less than an ambush, I was going to have to channel my inner Billings Girl. If I had one.

"I don't want to talk about that," I said for the tenth time.

For the tenth time, the reporter ignored me.

"How did it make you feel? Not only had you lost your boyfriend to a very violent death, but to know that your new boyfriend might have been responsible . . ."

Her digital recorder sat on the arm of her chair, its red light glaring at me. She leaned forward, holding a mechanical pencil poised over her notebook. Her dark hair fell over her tiny-framed glasses, but she didn't push it away. Her brow creased in faux concern as the photographer snapped a rapid-fire series of photographs, clearly capturing the slow demise of my spirits. Against the wall, the dean leaned back, his index finger crooked around his lips as he stared at the floor.

"I knew he wasn't responsible," I said through my teeth.

Next to me, Cheyenne and Trey shifted in their seats.

"You knew. You knew for absolute, one hundred percent certain," she said dubiously.

"I never doubted him," I said firmly.

"Then who do you think *did* do it?"

"All right, this interview is over," Dean Marcus announced.

Thank God. I was wondering if he was ever going to put an end to this. Cheyenne had said I wouldn't have to talk about Thomas if I didn't want to, and yet that was all this woman had asked me about. That and nothing else.

"I have a right to ask these questions, Dean," the reporter said.

"You're here to do a profile of the school and students, not an exposé on Thomas Pearson's murder, a topic which your paper has already covered exhaustively," the dean said, holding out a hand toward the door. "This young lady has already been through enough."

The reporter glanced at me. I tried to look pathetic so she'd leave me alone. At the moment it wasn't that much of a stretch.

"Fine," the reporter groused, rolling her eyes. She got up, gathering her oversize bag and recorder. "I've got enough for my piece."

"Good. Please feel free to call me if you have any further questions," the dean suggested, ushering her out. He walked her through his outer office, where Ms. Lewis-Hanneman sat at her computer, typing away. I wondered if she was really working or if she was just trying to look busy for the reporters.

"I'm so sorry about that, Reed," Cheyenne whispered to me as we brought up the rear. "She promised the dean she wouldn't ask anything too personal."

"It's all right," I told her. "She's just doing her job."

But if I'd known where her car was, I'd have let all the air out of her tires right then.

Just before the dean and the reporter got to the door, it burst open and Dash barreled in, breathless. For a moment everyone froze. It was obvious to the world that he had a huge announcement to make. He took one look at the reporter and cleared his throat.

"Hey. How's everyone doing?" he asked awkwardly.

"Fine, Mr. McCafferty. Thank you for stopping by to ask," the dean replied. His hand was on the small of the reporter's back as if he was more than ready to shove her out the door if he needed to.

"McCafferty. Dash McCafferty, right?" the reporter said, her eyes lighting up. "What's going on?"

"Nothing," Dash replied. "I just . . . came over to tell Trey that we're starting our study group an hour early. Are you guys done here?"

"Yes. We are," the dean said, even as the reporter opened her mouth to protest. "Mr. Jackson, would you kindly help me escort Ms. Vasquez and her colleague to the gates?"

"Absolutely, Dean Marcus," Scat said, emerging from a chair in the corner.

The reporter protested, but Scat had her out of there in five seconds, closing the door behind them.

"What is it?" I asked Dash.

"They found Blake," Dash said.

Ms. Lewis-Hanneman stopped typing but otherwise didn't move. Somehow I got the feeling she was not all that surprised by this revelation.

"No way," Cheyenne said.

"Where was he?" I asked.

"At the family's house in Bermuda," Dash said. "His parents sent a neighbor by to check, and he'd been there for a few days."

"It took them that long to think of their house in Bermuda?" Trey asked.

"It's not their only vacation home," Dash said. "They had to check all of them."

"So what's the deal?" Cheyenne asked. "Did he turn himself in?"

"Well, yeah. He's already been brought back for questioning, but he's maintaining his innocence," Dash said, sounding very official. "But who knows? Hopefully we'll finally get to the bottom of this."

Cheyenne took a deep breath and blew it out, shaking her head. "Well, we should get to dinner, I suppose," she said, checking her gold watch. She probably wanted to get there ASAP so that she could share this dish with everyone before they had a chance to hear it from someone else. "Coming, Reed?"

I glanced over at Ms. Lewis-Hanneman. Her fingers sat motionless on her keyboard.

"I'll be there in a minute," I told her. "I have something to ask the dean when he gets back."

"Okay. Thanks again for doing this," she said, reaching out to quickly squeeze my arm.

She and Trey walked out, and I had to smile. Cheyenne was so unlike Noelle. Noelle would have been suspicious and wanted to know what business I had with the dean. Either that or she would have smiled knowingly as if she already *knew* what business I had with the dean. Cheyenne had no interest. It was kind of refreshing.

Dash shot me a questioning look and I waved at him to go, which he did. Also refreshing.

"Are you okay?" I asked Ms. Lewis-Hanneman as soon as I was sure we were alone.

"I already knew," she said. "Blake's lawyer called me this morning."

"What did he say?" I asked, approaching her desk.

"He said that Blake left the country because of me. Like he wouldn't be in this mess if I wasn't such a coldhearted bitch."

"He said that?"

"No. But he was very good at implying it," she said with a small smirk. "Like I didn't feel guilty enough already."

"So . . . what? Blake was trying to get away from you or something?"

"Or something. I never told you this, but after Josh was arrested, I stopped taking Blake's calls. I didn't know what to do. Seeing him when we knew what we knew . . . it just seemed too complicated. I needed a break."

"I don't get it," I said. "What does that have to do with Blake going to Bermuda?"

"His lawyer says he just had to get away. He was heartbroken. He left the country because I was avoiding him, not because he was on the run." She picked up a bunch of papers and knocked them repeatedly against the desk to straighten them. Then knocked them a few extra times. "So it's all my fault he looks so guilty. Isn't that fab?"

"So you think he's innocent now," I stated.

She leveled me with a glare. "I know he's innocent. I can't believe I ever thought he wasn't."

I took a deep breath. It was a convenient story, but I wasn't convinced. I'd seen the ire that the very mention of Thomas raised in Blake. I could so easily imagine him losing control and doing something awful to Thomas. But I couldn't say that. Not to her.

"What's he telling the police?" I asked.

"He's keeping our secret," she said with a wry look. Like she couldn't believe he was still doing that for her—that he still cared. "The official party line is that he was broken up over Thomas's death and needed to get away."

Nice. He was using his brother's murder to make himself look more sympathetic. This guy was rich.

"His lawyer says I'm probably going to have to give a deposition, which basically means my life as I know it is over," she said. She shook her head and stared past me at the window. "I just keep thinking, if only we hadn't picked *that* night to get together. Blake would have been at Columbia, I would have been at home. . . . None of this would be happening."

She lost it a little then and snatched a tissue from the box on her desk. My heart went out to her, but I had no idea what to say. I knew how she felt. How many "if onlys" had I pondered since the beginning of the year? Hundreds? Thousands?

"I'm sorry. You shouldn't have to listen to this," she said, toying with the tissue. "It's just, you're the only person who knows the whole story, and if I don't talk to someone . . ."

"It's okay," I said. "I don't know if it'll make you feel any better, but you did the right thing. You couldn't let Josh sit in jail for something he didn't do."

She nodded. "I know."

"And I'm sure the lawyers will do everything they can to keep your name from getting out. I watch the news. They do this stuff all the time, right?"

She nodded again.

"The bottom line is, if Blake did do it, he needs to face up to it," I said.

"He didn't do it," she said firmly.

My jaw clenched. I realized then that I wanted Blake to be guilty. I wanted to be able to blame someone. I wanted this all to be over so that we could actually move on. So that someone could finally be punished for taking Thomas's life. For causing all this misery. But looking back at me were the eyes of a girl who wanted to believe more than anything that the guy she loved was a good guy. And I knew how that felt too.

"Well, then he needs this opportunity to clear his name," I said calmly. "Either way, it's better for everyone that he's back. It's the only way we're going to find out what happened."

She took a deep breath. "You're right. Thanks."

It felt like the moment for me to go, but I didn't want to move until she told me to.

"You know, Reed, you're kind of an old soul," she said finally.

A smile jumped to my lips. "Fifteen going on forty. My dad's been saying that since I was little. First I was eight going on forty, then ten. . . ."

"Well, it's refreshing around here," she said. "None of the kids who go here ever have to grow up, but you're already there. Thanks for listening."

"No problem," I told her.

I took that as my cue and walked out, closing the door softly behind me. I wished her the best. I truly did. She seemed like a cool, if slightly misguided, person. But I wondered if she'd thank me so sincerely, if she'd think I was so very mature, if she knew that in the back of my mind I was hoping against hope I'd see her boyfriend fry.

THE WAY IT WAS

The crowd on the circle was unusually boisterous that night. The air was crisp and clear and once again hundreds of stars winked overhead. It was as if a huge leaden blanket had been lifted off the campus. Blake was in custody. And we were all willing to believe that this horrible chapter had officially been closed. The worst was behind us.

"Who wants to get started early?" Kiran trilled, pulling a champagne bottle out from under her coat. As always she couldn't have cared less if any adults happened to be watching. Of course, the only people watching us were students in the three underclassmen dorms on the circle. Dozens of faces were pressed to the windows behind us, on the inside, looking out.

A few people cheered and Kiran popped the bottle open, letting the foam spill out onto the cobblestones at her feet. Already half-sloshed, she chugged from the bottle before passing it on to Trey and the boys. Ariana shook her head but smiled, and even Noelle laughed, cuddling back into Dash's arms. Walt Whittaker took out a handkerchief and wiped the bottle before drinking from it; then Gage made a big show of running his tongue all around the mouth before sucking down half the contents.

"Gage, man! You are so disgusting," Josh grimaced as everyone laughed and "eewww"ed.

"You are wrong, my friend! All the girls wanna suck my spit!" Gage said with a cackle, offering the bottle up.

"Ugh. That is just *so* unsanitary." Cheyenne grimaced, waving him away.

"I'll take it," Kiran said. She grabbed the bottle and took a swig and everyone "eew"ed again.

"God, Kiran. There will be plenty of germ-free bottles when we get there," Cheyenne said.

"Now where's the fun in that?" Kiran asked, drinking some more.

With each laugh, I felt lighter and lighter.

"It's good to be back," Josh said in my ear, pulling me to him.

My heart went all warm and gooey. "It's good to have you back."

A pair of headlights lit up the trees and Cheyenne squealed. "The cars are here!"

Two huge stretch SUVs rolled up the hill and somehow made the tight turn onto the circle. I had never seen anything like them before in my life. They were longer than buses, with huge tinted windows, and tires the size of a front door.

"Now that's how I roll!" Gage shouted, flinging open the door of the first limo before the driver could even get out. He got inside, kicked back, and started playing with the stereo, while the rest of us all tried to figure out who was going in which car.

"Let's hang back," Josh said, holding my hand.

"Why?" I asked as Ariana, Kiran, and Noelle ducked into Gage's limo. He stared after them and I realized. "You don't want to be in her limo."

Josh sighed. "I just . . . The less time I spend around that girl, the better."

Okay, this was no good. First Thomas hated the Billings Girls and now Josh? I had to fix this somehow or I was going to be spending the rest of the year running interference.

"Josh—"

He turned around and headed for the other car, but the driver closed the door right in front of him.

"Sorry, sir. All full," he said, holding up his hand. "There's room in the first car."

Josh's shoulders slumped.

"Come on," I said quietly. "It's just a short car ride. You can handle it."

"Hollis! Let's go, man!" Dash shouted, sticking his head out of the limo.

Josh turned to me, took a deep breath, and managed a smile. He lifted my hand and kissed it.

"You're right. It doesn't matter. All that matters is that I'm here."

"Couldn't have said it better myself."

We settled into the limo on the opposite end from Noelle and Dash. Somehow Cheyenne, Trey, and Rose had ended up with us as well. I would have thought Cheyenne would want to stay as far away from Noelle as possible tonight, just to avoid any unpleasantness, but maybe I'd underestimated her. Maybe she wanted to show how very much she wasn't affected.

Josh hooked his arm around me and cuddled me into his side, and I resolved to stop thinking about the politics of Billings. Noelle and Dash were holding hands and whispering to each other. Kiran and Ariana were laughing over some shared story. Cheyenne and Trey were smooching, and Whittaker and Rose were chatting about their upcoming trips for the holidays. And we were all being whisked off campus to a private party while the rest of campus studied or slept or hung out in their common rooms watching DVDs and playing video games. Everything was getting back to the way it had been before. Everything was going to be okay.

THE PALACE

During the course of the ride, everyone kept shifting and moving around. Whispering, gossiping, checking out one another's jewelry and hair. Somehow Noelle and Dash ended up next to me and Josh. I sat in the center of the foursome with Noelle, while Josh pressed his knee into the door and stared out the window away from us. I could feel his tension and hoped we would be arriving soon just so that he could breathe again.

"I still can't believe we're doing this," Noelle muttered. She whipped out a platinum compact and checked her hair in the mirror. Turned her face from side to side. "It's going to be so lame."

I glanced across the limo at Cheyenne, who was laughing as Rose sang along to the song on the radio.

"Don't stress. She can't hear me," Noelle said, snapping the mirror closed. "Not that I'd care if she did."

"Just relax, Noelle. It'll be fun no matter where we're going, as long as we're all together," Dash said lightly.

"Okay, Tiny Tim. Whatever you say," Noelle shot back.

I laughed and Josh tensed even further. Apparently he didn't even appreciate me laughing at her jokes.

"Just look at this," Noelle said, scooting forward on her seat so she could see out the window on Dash's side. "We're in the middle of Dorothy land. Farmhouse. Farmhouse. Silo. Farmhouse. Oh, look! Cows! I knew we were going tipping!"

That one Cheyenne heard. She glared at all of us for a moment before deciding to ignore it. She returned her attention to Rose.

"She said there was going to be champagne. It's not like she's totally clueless," Dash said under his breath.

"Well, there'd better be a lot of it if she doesn't want this to be the disaster of the century," Noelle grumbled. "Where is this place, anyway, Martin? Are you taking us to Canada? Because I don't do flannel."

"We're almost there," Cheyenne replied, blithely smoothing her coat over her knees.

The limo took a turn and whatever small amount of light there had been was gone. Curious, I scooted forward to look out Josh's window. There was nothing outside but the night sky and the trees, crowding in on all sides. We were on a road that appeared to be one lane. If anyone came at us from the other direction, someone would have to pull off into the dirt. "Middle of nowhere" was the phrase that came to mind.

"Maybe she's taking us to her coven," Noelle theorized. "Maybe we're all going to be sacrificed."

"That could be exciting," Kiran put in.

"Seriously. It's like *Children of the Corn* out there. Where the hell are we?"

She wasn't actually concerned, just obnoxious. The car turned again and I could feel the bump of cobblestones or bricks under the tires.

"We're here!" Cheyenne announced.

Suddenly the car was flooded with light. Josh perked up and Dash whistled. Everyone gathered at the windows now, sitting up on their knees to face out. We were on a long driveway that was flanked on either side by huge sparklers stuck into the ground, spitting white fire into the sky. There were hundreds of them, sparking and cracking, lighting the way to the house.

"What the . . . ?"

The house. The house was not a house. It was a palace. It stretched out for what seemed like miles and rose up toward the sky with turrets and spires. On the second floor alone there were at least a dozen balconies with sliding doors. Light poured from every window, and each one was adorned with a classic wreath and red bow. There was a fountain in the center of the circular drive, and in the middle was a huge Christmas tree, all lit up and decorated with crystal ornaments.

"What is this, Versailles?" I said under my breath.

Josh chuckled and put his arm around me, finally relaxed. "So much for the sucky cow-tipping party, huh, Noelle?"

She shot him a death glare as the limo pulled up next to a

couple dozen other cars that were already parked in front of the house.

"Huh," Noelle said. "Looks like there are already some people here, Martin."

Cheyenne's face went ashen, and I knew. Everyone knew. Something was wrong, and whatever it was, Noelle had planned it. Her observation was not the product of surprise. All at once I heard the music pumping through the open front door.

"What the hell is going on?" Cheyenne blurted.

She grabbed for the door handle and tumbled out before the limo had even come to a complete stop. Trey quickly followed. We all looked at Noelle, who was barely suppressing a grin. She stared back at us, arranging her face into the picture of innocence.

"What?" she asked, eyebrows raised.

I shook my head at her and chased after Cheyenne.

OUT-SCHEMED

Stepping inside Cheyenne's summer home was like stepping into a museum. Everything was huge. The Croton High gym could have fit in the entry hall. The Christmas tree set into the crook of the winding stairs was big enough to grace Rockefeller Center. The mirrors were huge, the paintings were huge, the chandelier was frightening. I didn't even want to stand under the thing.

"This place is sick," Josh whispered as he shed his coat.

"It's a summer home," I said, wondering what the home they actually lived in looked like. "They only stay here during the summer."

"Yeah, so who decorated it for the holidays?" Rose wondered.

"Girl with money like this just has to snap her fingers and the staff of thousands takes care of it," Dash said, folding his coat and scarf over his arm. "Did anyone know Cheyenne was this loaded?"

"Not I, but I officially have a whole new respect for the girl,"

Gage said. "She could keep me in the manner to which I've become accustomed."

Noelle rolled her eyes and walked across the room, her heels clicking on the marble floor. Somewhere beyond the foyer there were voices and music. I hadn't even noticed it in all the awe. But now I saw that Noelle was heading for it and that Cheyenne and Trey stood hand in hand at one of several sets of open double doors. I hurried to join them.

Cheyenne's face was all surprise as she took in the crowd in what I could only assume was her living room. Though how anyone could actually live among so much white without constantly staining something was beyond me. There were white throw rugs on the floor, square couches of white velvet, white high-backed chairs, and white pillows. Lounging on and around all the luxe furniture were at least fifty people, talking, drinking, and laughing. The doors at the side of the room were open to the outside, and I could see the lights on over an outdoor courtyard. A fire blazed in the huge fireplace, and waitresses circulated the room in black turtlenecks and slim pants, like a dozen Audrey Hepburns come to life. I recognized none of the guests, but could tell from their clothing and their demeanor that they were of the same class as the rest of the Easton students. Still, where had they come from? Did Cheyenne even know who these people were?"Oh, look!" Noelle said happily, shoving past the rest of us. "There's Ennis!"

She grabbed a tall boy by the arm and dragged him toward us without so much as a greeting. He wore a blazer, shirt, and tie and looked like he was auditioning to be in a movie about 1950s prep schools, all fresh-faced and handsome. Cheyenne dropped Trey's hand and folded her arms across her chest.

"Ennis Thatcher, this is everyone. Everyone, this is Ennis, Cheyenne's boyfriend," Noelle announced with an utterly spiteful grin. "Ennis, this is Trey Prescott—Cheyenne's *date*."

My heart stopped for Cheyenne. Kiran snorted behind me. Noelle was good. She paid attention. She really knew how to hit a person where it hurt.

Ennis flicked a look at Trey, like he wasn't quite sure what to make of him. He shifted his feet.

"Hey, Cheyenne," Ennis said.

"Ennis," she said. She was as pale as the snow outside. "What are you doing here?"

"Oh, did I forget to tell you?" Noelle asked, hand to chest. "I invited all of your Barton friends. I posted the invite on their school website. I thought it was the least I could do after you saved our holiday party. And I knew you'd just be dying to see Ennis again."

Cheyenne cast a sidelong glance at Noelle. I couldn't tell what she was thinking. Possibly her mind was a total blank after being so utterly blindsided.

"Hope you don't mind, Shy," Ennis said. "It was kind of cold outside, so I used the key code and let everyone in."

"Of course I don't mind," Cheyenne said, recovering quickly. "It's not like I want my guests standing outside freezing to death."

Ennis gave her a tight smile, then looked at Trey. Here it came. The throwdown. The "What the hell are you doing here with a date?" Noelle's moment of triumph and Cheyenne's moment of defeat. I held my breath.

"Hey, Trey. It's nice to finally meet you," Ennis said, reaching out his hand.

I felt like the whole room had just tilted and then slammed back into place. Wait. What? "Nice to finally meet you"?

"You too, man. I've heard a lot about you," Trey replied.

They shook hands. Right there under Noelle's nose. I had never seen her look so nonplussed.

"What?" Noelle blurted. "Ennis, did you hear what I said? Trey is Cheyenne's *date.*"

"I heard you," Ennis replied, pushing his hands into his pockets. There were patches of pink on his cheeks, but otherwise he seemed fine. "And I'm sorry to have to correct you, but Cheyenne and I are no longer together."

I thought Noelle's jaw was going to actually fall from her face. A high-pitched sound came from the back of her throat. A sound she immediately regretted making as her mouth snapped shut and she turned royal purple.

"You—," she fumed at Cheyenne. As if Cheyenne was the one who had attempted to do something awful here.

Cheyenne simply smiled, her eyes gleaming mischievously. "Oh. Did *I* forget to tell *you* that Ennis and I broke up, Noelle?" she said, lifting her hand to her chest the same way Noelle had.

Josh chuckled and Natasha hid a smile. Badly.

"Nice try, Noelle, but everyone here knows about everyone else," Cheyenne added. "Your *cute* little plan was sort of a waste of time, no?"

"Wait a minute. At Billings that day, you said—"

Cheyenne's brow creased in an overly exaggerated way. "Oh, right! I guess when I told you I wasn't ball-and-chained to my man, I should have also explained that Ennis was no longer the man in question. But it was so much more fun, you finding out this way, don't you think?"

Noelle looked as if she were choking on her tongue.

"And P.S., I invited everyone from Barton before you did. All you've done is get them here a little early, so thanks for that."

Josh, Natasha, Rose, and a few others laughed. The entire world shifted before my eyes. Noelle was speechless, Cheyenne triumphant. Someone had actually out-schemed Noelle. It was actually possible.

In that moment I felt proud of Cheyenne. Proud to know her. The universe didn't revolve around Noelle Lange, and Cheyenne had just proven it.

She waved to someone across the room, then reached for my hand. "Come on, Reed, there are some people I want you to meet."

"Me?" I asked, surprised.

"Everyone already knows everyone else, pretty much," she said, giddy with her victory. "You too, Josh." She tilted her head. "Let's go."

Josh couldn't have been happier to get away from Noelle and her klatch of supporters. He handed our coats to Dash, then grabbed a couple of champagne flutes off a passing waiter's tray as we wove through the crowd. Several people greeted Cheyenne with warm hellos and pecks on the cheek. She was clearly very popular among this Barton crowd, which made me wonder why she didn't go there instead of Easton. Sure she was in Billings, but she didn't have nearly this many friends at school as she had here.

"Astrid! Hey!"

A beautiful girl with dark, almond-shaped eyes and short dark hair leaned forward for a hug and a double-cheek air kiss. She wore a short-sleeved fuzzy sweater in aqua blue over a silky white dress and had a funky antique brooch in her hair. There was a rhinestone above her left eyebrow, and her glittery eye makeup made her look like a wood sprite from a Shakespeare play.

"There you are, love!" she said with a British accent. "We've been wondering when you'd turn up."

"Sorry to be late," Cheyenne said. "Astrid, I'd like you to meet Reed Brennan and Josh Hollis. This is Astrid Chou and her boyfriend, Cole Roget."

"No way! I've been absolutely *dying* to meet you," Astrid cried. She wrapped me up in a soft yet firm hug, and I breathed in the scent of a million flowers.

"You have?" I asked, laughing.

"Are you joking? You two are, like, famous!" Astrid replied. "Aren't they, Cole?"

"Probably not for reasons you'd want to be," Cole said kindly, leaning forward to shake both our hands. He was a compact guy with square shoulders and shaggy dark hair. "Congratulations on being exonerated, man."

"Thanks," Josh said, clearing his throat. He took a sip of his champagne.

"And you probably want to talk about anything other than that," Cole said, putting his hand in his pocket. He tipped his glass of scotch toward Josh. "So tell me, Josh. What's your thing?"

"My thing?" Josh asked.

"Cole is a brilliant conversationalist," Astrid announced, her eyes gleaming with pride. "It's a dying art, really. He can talk about anything. Just tell him what your thing is."

"Sports. Art. Literature. Politics. Architecture. What's your thing?" Cole asked, sipping his drink.

Josh and I looked at each other and laughed. These people were quirky, but in a good way. Very unlike anyone I had ever met. Josh shrugged one shoulder and decided to go with it.

"All right, then. My thing is art," he said.

"Beautiful!" Cole said, lifting an arm to place his hand on Josh's back. He led him toward a set of chairs by the fire. "What do you think of the new installation at MoMA? Brilliantly outré or just plain crass?"

Astrid, Cheyenne, and I watched them go, and I couldn't stop smiling.

"I knew those two would hit it off," Cheyenne said.

"I think this is exactly what he needed. Distraction is good," I told her. "Thanks, Cheyenne."

"Of course," Cheyenne said.

"All right, enough of the Hallmark moment," Astrid said, grabbing my hand and tugging. "Let's go to the bar and get pissed."

THE FIRE PIT

I had never worn a bikini before in my life, yet somehow I found myself standing outside in the freezing December air, wrapped in a towel, with nothing underneath but a tiny black thing with strings at my hips and tied in a bow behind my neck. Twelve friends and semistrangers stared up at me from the hot tub.

"Okay, it's about negative fifteen degrees out here," I said, clinging to the towel.

"That's why you want to get into the hot tub straight away," Astrid said.

She, by the way, was naked under there, as were a few of the other girls. Apparently they had been here drinking for a *while* before we showed up. Oddly, none of the guys seemed to be the least bit fazed by all the skin.

"Go on, Reed! Take it off!" Astrid cheered.

All the guys, including Josh, hooted and hollered. It was now or never. Now, or look like the biggest prude of the century. I dropped the towel and stepped directly into the hot water, immersing myself up to my neck before anyone could get a good look at my almost naked self.

"See? That wasn't so bad, was it?" Cheyenne asked.

She was wearing a suit too, of course. And so was Josh. As long as I had people on either side of me who had clothes on, I was cool.

"Thanks for letting me borrow this," I said.

"You can keep it if you want," Cheyenne said, taking a sip from a bottle of water. "I have dozens."

"Yeah. I noticed. All bikinis," I said, reaching back to fix a slight wedgie.

"We're not gonna have these bodies forever, Reed," Astrid said. "May as well enjoy them while we do."

"So, Cole, when do you leave for France?" Cheyenne asked.

"Second week of January," Cole said. "I've got so much to do."

"Are you going on vacation?" I asked.

"No, no. Barton has an exchange program with a school just outside Paris," Cole explained. "Every year five juniors get to go study the French classics. This year I was lucky enough to be selected."

"Luck had nothing to do with it," Astrid said, placing her champagne glass down on the bricks so she could ruffle his hair. "I am going to miss you, though. Barton is going to be quite dull without you around."

"Please. Barton is never dull," Astrid's friend Leah said. "It's all drama, all the time."

"Please. You don't know drama until you've been at Easton," Cheyenne joked.

"She's right. We've cornered the market on that," Josh put in wryly.

"But it's over now," I said. "Next semester I think things are going to be very normal."

"Wishful thinking," Rose put in with a small snort.

"You should transfer to Barton, Reed. Not only do we have less drama, we could really use you on the football pitch," Astrid said with a wink.

"You play?" I asked.

"I'm forced to," Astrid replied. "But I do remember watching you from the sidelines in September. Very impressive. Perhaps Coach would give me a pass next year if I could convince you to defect."

Right. We had pretty much crushed Barton in our match earlier in the season.

"No, no, no. Reed is staying right where she is," Josh said, slinging his arm over my shoulder.

My heart swooped and I cuddled closer to him. "I have no problem with that."

"Aw! Look at these two!" Astrid said. "Could they be any more precious?"

Josh and I looked at each other and grinned. It was amazing how much more I appreciated moments like this, now that they'd been so close to being gone for good. He leaned in for a kiss and as our lips met, my cell phone beeped. I grabbed it up from the circle of cells and PDAs that surrounded the hot tub. The text message read:

MEET UPSTAIRS. SOUTH WING. 5 DOOR LEFT.

U DONT WANT 2 MISS THIS!!!

My chest constricted. A secret text message from Noelle. How long had it been since I'd gotten one of those? I felt the familiar tingle of curiosity and looked up at the house, as if I'd see one of them beckoning to me from a window.

"It's Noelle, isn't it?" Cheyenne asked suspiciously. "What are they doing?"

"Nothing. They're just inside by the pool table and they want me to come in," I lied.

Josh pulled my hand toward him and read the message. His face went hard. Oh, God. He wasn't going to tell Cheyenne where they actually were, was he?

"What's with her?" he spat. "It's like she says jump and everyone around her is supposed to say, 'Cool! Into what fire pit?'"

Everyone laughed, but my stomach felt tight. I wanted to go. There was no denying it. Even after everything that had happened, Noelle's pull was undeniable. What were they doing in the fifth room on the left of the south wing? Something fabulous? Something bad? Something fabulously bad? I was dying to find out.

Part of me hated that they still had this effect on me, but they did.

"What?" Josh said quietly, noticing my contemplation. "You're not actually thinking about meeting up with her, are you?"

"Well—"

"Reed, come on. You don't have to do everything she says. Don't let her ruin this."

His blue eyes searched mine. Sincere. Caring. Trusting. They were so full of purity, just looking at them made me feel guilty.

He was right. I knew he was. I didn't have to go running every time Noelle told me to. If I had learned anything over the past few weeks, it was that I was perfectly capable of standing up to her. But this time she wasn't ordering me to do anything. She was inviting me. I could easily turn her down. The question was, did I want to?

The answer, according to my excitedly pounding heart, was no.

"It'll just be a couple of minutes," I said, pushing myself up. The hot water sluiced from my bare skin and the cold air hit me full force.

"Oh, boo!" Astrid grinned.

"Sorry. I'll be back." I grabbed my towel and scurried for the pool house, where we'd all left our clothes. Josh, after the briefest hesitation, was right behind me. He closed the door behind us and I grabbed my skirt and sweater—well, Kiran's skirt and sweater—off the couch in the living area and headed for one of the bedrooms. That's right. The pool house had two bedrooms, a sauna, a changing area with four changing rooms and a bar. Roughly the size of some of the homes back in Croton.

"You're not really going up there, are you?" Josh demanded, whipping a towel from a hook in one of the changing rooms. He wrapped it around his shoulders as water dripped from his hair.

"They're probably just exploring the house," I said. "It's no big deal."

I closed the slatted door to the bedroom behind me and quickly shed the wet bathing suit, then dried myself off as best I could. Every second I expected the cell phone to beep again, asking where the hell I was. I found, to my amazement, that I was excited by the idea rather than petrified. Things had definitely changed.

"It's a big deal to me!" Josh said through the door. "Reed, Noelle is . . . she's . . . she's evil!" he blurted. "And you're at her beck and call! You're at evil's beck and call."

I pulled my skirt and sweater on, then opened the door. "Josh, she's just a girl with a power complex. She's not evil."

"I'm not so sure about that," he said. "Reed, she thought I was a murderer. She thought I was some deranged psycho and she called the police on me! She even almost turned you against me!"

"Yeah, but she didn't," I said, as I shoved my feet into my shoes.

"That is so not the point and you know it," Josh said. "You're about to walk out on me and go hang out with a girl who tried to have me locked up for life."

"Don't be so dramatic," I blurted.

His entire face contorted. "Excuse me?"

The second the words were out of my mouth, I regretted them. It was just that I was so sick of the drama. So sick of the confusion and the exhaustion and the sorrow. It was over now. Why couldn't he see that? I just wanted to be with my friends. Yes, they had their faults, but if anything had been proven tonight, it was that they weren't untouchable. They weren't unfazeable. Cheyenne Martin had dished it to Noelle earlier, and Noelle had just eaten it. They weren't that different from the rest of us.

"That's not what I meant," I said. "It's just . . . it's not Noelle's fault. She was just trying to figure out what happened to Thomas. Just like everyone else was. She just wanted an explanation."

"Yeah, and she conveniently blamed Psycho Hollis," he said, his jaw clenching.

"Josh—"

"No. You know what? If you want her to be your friend so badly, fine," he said, throwing up a hand as he turned away from me. "But if you go up there, don't bother coming back down."

All the air rushed out of the room. "What?"

"I'm serious, Reed. I don't like that girl. I don't want to be around her. And if you want to be around her, then you clearly don't want to be around me," he said, his eyes flashing in a way I'd never seen before.

I stood there, staring at him, unable to believe what I was hearing.

"I'm not very good with ultimatums, Josh," I said shakily.

"Yeah, well, I don't usually drop them," he said flatly. "But it looks like I just did."

"Well," I said, fighting back the sting of tears, "have a good night then."

Then, much to both his shock and mine, I turned my back on him and walked out.

COUTURE REVENGE

I found my way upstairs quickly, running on pure adrenaline. Who did Josh think he was? I knew he'd been through a lot, but didn't he realize how much I'd been through trying to help him? If he trusted me, if he respected me, he could never talk to me like that. Just when we were having such a sweet, romantic time, he had to go and ruin it with a ridiculous demand.

Or one could say *I* had ruined it, by running off to meet up with the Billings Girls.

I slowed down as I reached the first door in the south wing, feeling suddenly nauseated. Had I just chosen Noelle over Josh? Had that really just happened? But no. It shouldn't have to be one or the other, should it? I could have just come up here for a little while and gone right back down to Josh. He was the one who'd said he couldn't be around me. It was all him. Wasn't it?

Down the hallway, I could see a shaft of light coming from the open door to one of the rooms. I could hear my friends' laughter. There was still time to turn back. To figure out a way to fix this.

No, no, no. I was not going to go back down there with my tail between my legs. If I was going to start standing up for myself, it couldn't just be against Noelle. I had to stand up for myself in every aspect of my life. And that meant standing my ground with Josh. I took a deep breath and strolled the rest of the way.

When I pushed open the door to the tremendous bedroom, the first thing I saw was Kiran draped across the gold satin sheets in a green ball gown fit for a princess. She had a thick necklace of stunning diamonds and emeralds around her neck and a huge bauble on one of her hands. Ariana stood at the foot of the bed in a gorgeous, slinky, blue sheath, snapping photos with Kiran's camera phone.

"There you are, Reed!"

Noelle came up behind me and flung a hanger over my shoulder, holding a purple dress up against my body. It had a full skirt that looked as if it were made out of a thousand purple feathers.

"We thought that this would be *perfect* for you!"

"What took you so long?" Ariana asked, arching one eyebrow.

"I got lost," I lied, taking the hanger from Noelle, who was wearing a red-and-black gown right out of *Moulin Rouge*. Behind her a closet the size of my house was open, and gowns of all colors were strewn on the floor and on the benches inside the closet. Dozens of pairs of shoes had been pulled off their shelves and were knocked over on the floor. A drawer full of sparkling jewelry sat open, its contents having obviously been pawed through. "What the hell are you guys doing?"

"Cheyenne's stepmother is a collector," Noelle said. She disappeared inside the closet and came out with a tiara on her head.

"A collector of clothes?" I asked, dropping the purple dress on the bed next to Kiran.

"No, silly! A collector of couture," Kiran said, rolling over the luxurious bedspread as she giggled. "I love this bed! I want to marry this bed!"

"You are very drunk," I pointed out.

"Nice to state the obvious," Noelle said, checking her reflection in the mirror.

"What's the matter, Reed?" Ariana asked. "You're all tense."

I blew out a sigh. Might as well tell them. They would find out sooner or later. "I just had a big fight with Josh."

"Oh. That's too bad," Ariana said with a small frown.

"Well, you know what the best revenge is, don't you?" Kiran asked, grabbing one of the bedposts and hoisting herself up to her knees.

I blinked.

Kiran reached behind her and snatched up the purple dress. "The best revenge is couture!"

"Put it on!" Noelle cheered, grabbing for a bottle of champagne.

"It will look incredible on you," Ariana added.

"Come on, Reed. You know you want it," Kiran said, looking at me through heavy lashes.

Funny. One minute people were cheering for me to take it off, now they were cheering for me to put it on.

"Please, Reed?" Kiran trilled. "Pretty please?" She pouted and batted her lashes crazily.

"Fine." I laughed, rolling my eyes, and took the dress from her. Knowing how they mocked modesty, I quickly stripped right in front of them and stepped into the dress. Noelle came around and did up the side zipper for me.

"Well. That was made for you," Ariana said appreciatively.

"Actually, it was made for Rinnan Hearst, but who's counting?" Kiran said, jumping down from the bed.

"Rinnan Hearst. Why do I know that name?"

"Omigod. You don't know who Rinnan Hearst is?" Kiran almost choked.

I started for the mirror, but Noelle held me back. "No! Hair and jewelry first. It's better if you can get the full effect. Ariana?"

Ariana walked into the closet and came back with a pair of diamond-studded chopsticks, which Noelle used to put my hair into a quick updo. Then they placed a huge yellow diamond necklace around my neck. It was very heavy, and the jewels were cold against my skin.

"Rinnan Hearst is Cheyenne's stepmother," Ariana said, stepping back to check her work. "She's also been nominated for three Academy Awards."

Right. I'd seen her in a movie once. Though which one I had no idea. I had a vague mental picture of a tall woman with coffee-colored skin, dark eyes, and no body fat.

"Plus she's only, like, thirty," Kiran said, swigging from the champagne bottle.

"Or so she says," Noelle added coyly.

"Wait, why were you guys so surprised at the size of this house if Cheyenne's stepmother is a movie star?" I asked.

"Reed, you have got so much to learn," Kiran said. She threw her arms wide and some of the champagne sloshed out of the bottle. "This is not indie-movie-queen money. This is *old* money."

"What does Cheyenne's father do, exactly?" Ariana asked.

"No one's ever cared enough to find out for sure," Noelle said. "He's some kind of international business mogul."

"Well, I hope Rinnan's not too attached to him, because I wouldn't mind being wife number three," Kiran said with a cackle.

I balked. "Come on. Wouldn't Cheyenne's dad be kind of old for you?"

"Sweetie, I don't care if he's old or young, ugly or pretty. As long as he's financing the couture, he's fine by me," Kiran trilled.

"Hear, hear!" Noelle and Ariana both cheered before taking mouthfuls of champagne.

"Anyway, Reed, you are now wearing the exact outfit Ms. Rinnan Hearst wore when she lost at the Oscars for the third time," Ariana said with a smile.

Whoa. This dress had been down the red carpet at the Academy Awards? Even I could appreciate the fabulousness of that. Noelle finally let me go and I stepped in front of the mirror. The tension inside of me melted away. I really did look like a movie star.

"Okay, everyone! Get together!" Kiran said, grabbing the camera phone from Ariana.

Ariana and Noelle crowded in around me, striking ridiculous model-style posses. Hands on hips, butts jutted out, lips puckered. I mimicked them, laughing at myself as they draped their arms over me, pressed their cheeks to mine. It was all very silly and fun. An impromptu fashion show. It was the type of thing I always knew girls did on their own time, but I had never actually experienced. Of course, where I lived the clothes came from Forever 21, not the House of Chanel.

"Okay, people! Wardrobe change!" Kiran announced.

Noelle grabbed my hand and pulled me into the closet to select another dress. For the first time in days, I wasn't thinking about Thomas or Blake or Josh or anything else. For the first time in days, I was just having fun.

A PHOTO

Josh ignored me for the rest of the night. I didn't approach him, either. Whenever we were in a room together, I felt like there was a bungee cord between us trying to pull me over to him, but I resisted. I was angry. I was hurt. And there was no way I was apologizing first.

We took separate limos home, but they both pulled up at the same time. When I stepped out into the cold, Josh was standing a few yards away, staring at me. Noelle came out and huddled into me from behind, putting her chin on my shoulder. Josh's face went blank before he turned around and walked off alone.

There was a huge hole where my heart used to be.

"Screw him," Noelle said, slipping her arm through mine. "We had a good night. You can fix it in the morning."

"You're right," I said, shaking my hair back.

Dash came over and gave Noelle a quick good-night kiss before heading off in the direction of the guys' dorms. Then Kiran tripped over the curb into us and Ariana helped us get her standing up straight.

"Have you gotten your membership card from the Future Betty Ford's Inmate Club yet?" Noelle asked.

"Huh?" Kiran was confused.

Noelle rolled her eyes. "Forget it."

Together the four of us started up the cobblestone walk that would take us around my old dorm, Bradwell, and into the quad. Overhead the stars still twinkled and winked. Normally after a night like this the Billings Girls and the boys of Ketlar would have been rolling in as the sun came up, but the dean had stipulated an early night as part of his deal with Cheyenne and her dad. It was barely even one in the morning.

"Hey! Let's look at the pictures!" Kiran announced suddenly. She lifted her bag and attempted to open the clasp five times before it finally came free.

"Here. Let me," Noelle said.

She grabbed the bag and fished out the phone, which Kiran promptly snatched back. "You don't know how to work it."

"Fine," Noelle said, impatient. She looked at me and shook her head, and I laughed. Up ahead, the rest of the girls were crowding through the front door of Billings.

"Here! Look!" Kiran said.

All four of us huddled around her as we walked, the better to see the tiny screen. Kiran jabbed the arrow button with her thumb repeatedly, scrolling through the shots. There was one of me and

Noelle hugging. One of Ariana and Kiran lounging on the bed. One
of Noelle, Ariana, and me with our heads cut off, clearly taken by a
less-than-sober Kiran.

"You suck!" Noelle said, smacking Kiran's arm. "That should
have been a great shot."

"Hey! I'm a model, not a photographer," Kiran replied.

Ariana and I laughed.

There was Ariana in her blue gown, a shot of Noelle's tiara,
Kiran and me on the bed. Ariana, Noelle, me, Kiran, Noelle,
Ariana, me, and—

A naked torso. A guy's torso. Stretched and bound. A guy with a
black bag over his head, tied to some kind of pole. A blindfolded,
half-naked—

Thomas.

Everyone stopped moving. The world stopped moving.

"What—?" My vision blackened from the outside in, blocking
out everything until all I could see was that image. I knew Thomas's
body. Would know it anywhere. It was him. It was *him*.

The image shook in Kiran's hands. Her skin was actually gray.
"Omigod. Omigod."

She hit a bunch of buttons, but nothing worked. Nothing cleared
the horrifying image that was burning itself into every corner of my
mind.

"What *is* that!?" I shouted, backing away. The pain in my
stomach was so intense I doubled over. Ariana stared straight
ahead as if in shock. Kiran blubbered. Noelle, cool as ice, slowly

reached over and took the phone out of Kiran's hand. She clicked a few buttons.

"It's nothing," she said firmly. "It's gone."

"I'm sorry," Kiran blurted. Her whole body trembled. Even her eyes seemed to shake in their sockets. She gripped her own arms and backed away from Noelle and Ariana like she was afraid they might pounce. "I'm so, so sorry. I thought I deleted it. I thought—"

"Who the hell told you to take pictures?" Noelle demanded.

"I'm sorry. I'm sorry. We just thought . . . a goof. It was a goof. I thought—"

"Shut up," Ariana said through her teeth. I could see her jaw working. The anger she was smothering was boiling just below the surface.

Kiran was desperate. "But I thought I deleted it—"

"Shut up, Kiran."

"Ariana, please! It didn't seem like a big deal at the time! I just—"

"Shut the hell up!" Ariana roared.

Tears blurred my vision. This wasn't happening. This could not be happening. *Thomas. Thomas. Thomas.* He was half naked. His arms were lashed behind him. His head was covered. He couldn't see. There was no way he could see. Thomas was murdered. Thomas was *murdered.* And they had a picture of him. Like he was being tortured. Like *they* had—

"What did you do?" I heard myself say. My head was shaking. I couldn't focus. Tears streamed down my face. "What the hell did you do?"

Noelle took a step toward me. Nothing about her had changed. While Kiran deteriorated into a blathering mess and Ariana turned steely, Noelle was perfectly in control. She still held the phone, the screen now blank.

"Reed, calm down. It's not what you think."

"What do I *think*?" I practically screamed.

Maybe Josh was right. Maybe she was pure evil.

Ariana and Noelle looked around at the deserted campus as my voice echoed against the ancient walls. Kiran cried quietly into her velvet gloves.

"Okay . . . okay," Noelle said, holding a hand out. "We're going to explain. We're going to tell you exactly what happened, but you have to calm down."

"We don't have to explain a thing to her," Ariana snapped. Her fingers were curled into fists at her sides. She looked smaller somehow, but powerful. Like she'd pulled herself into her protective shell, primed for a fight.

Noelle ignored her. "Just calm down and listen to me, Reed."

Trembling from my very core, I somehow managed to reach into my coat pocket and pull out my cell phone. Noelle's expression changed for the first time. She looked at my phone as if it were a bomb. Something shifted inside of me and I found a tiny little bit of control. Something to grasp on to through all the bedlam roiling inside.

"You have five minutes," I said through my teeth. "Five minutes to convince me not to call the police."

Ariana glared at me. She wanted to punch me. I could tell from the malice in her eyes. Miss Manners herself, salivating to throw a right hook.

"Fine," she said. "But not here. We go inside."

"I'm not going anywhere with you. You ki—"

My throat closed up over the words and tears spilled out of my eyes.

"We didn't, Reed. I swear to you," Noelle said. "Please. You said you'd give us five minutes. Just please. Please, let's go inside."

She was begging me. Noelle Lange was standing there begging me. Her brown eyes were desperate, pleading. She was scared. She was scared and she needed me to believe her. I had never thought I'd see the day.

And in the end, that was what got me to follow them. Into Billings House. Into our home. Into a place I'd soon wish I'd never set foot inside at all.

THE WHOLE STORY

They killed Thomas. They *killed* Thomas.

I sat on the edge of Noelle's messy bed with that one thought repeating itself over and over and over again.

They killed Thomas. Killed him. Dead. He was dead because of my . . . my friends.

It was the only explanation. Why else would they have that picture? Why else would they all have freaked so badly at the sight of it? As I sat there, it all started to make sense. No wonder Noelle had brightened each time a new suspect had been brought into custody. Each time the blame was thrown on someone else, she was that much safer. And Kiran. She'd been all meek and edgy after Thomas's body had been found, but had returned to über-bitch form after Josh and then Blake had been arrested. Even Ariana had been in a weirdly good mood lately.

Why? Because they thought they'd gotten away with it. They thought they'd gotten away with murder.

I was going to be sick. Just tonight I had ditched Josh for these people. I had thought they were my friends. But they were murderers. Murderers.

Over in the corner Noelle and Ariana whispered, casting furtive glances in my direction every so often. Kiran sat on Noelle's desk chair, staring at a spot some three feet in front of her on the floor. Which one of them had actually done it? Which one of them had landed the blow that finally killed him?

And what the hell was I still doing here?

"That's it. I'm gone." I stood. I had thrown my coat off to keep myself from suffocating, but now I grabbed it from the bed and made for the door. Difficult to do without turning my back to them, but I did it. I wasn't taking my eyes off of them for a second.

"Reed! No," Noelle said.

I stopped. My hand was on the doorknob. All I had to do was turn it and run. "You said you would let us explain." Noelle took a couple of steps toward me. "Just sit down for five minutes."

My grip on the doorknob tightened. My fingers hurt. My palm hurt. Every single inch of me hurt.

"Why should I? We all know what happened," I spat.

"No. You don't," she said. "Let us at least tell the story and then if you still don't believe us, you can go tell whomever you want. We won't try to stop you."

I stared at her. At Ariana and her cool eyes. At Kiran, who was now looking at me, pleading silently.

I don't know if I really wanted to believe them, or if I just wanted to know—finally know once and for all—what had happened to Thomas that night. But whatever it was, something inside of me made me walk back to the bed. Made me sit down. Made me listen.

Noelle stood in front of me. She took a deep breath. "Okay. This is what really happened. Do you remember the night before Thomas disappeared? How we were all up in the woods?"

"Yes." Of course I remembered. I would remember every detail of those few days for the rest of my life.

"Do you remember how he treated you?" Ariana asked. "All those horrible things he said in front of everyone?"

My heart twisted and a wet sob welled up in my throat. I nodded.

"Well, we were all really pissed off after that little performance of his," Noelle said, starting to pace. "So we decided to teach him a lesson. You know, mess with his head a little bit. Show him that's no way to treat a Billings Girl."

"But I wasn't a Billings Girl then," I said.

"You were. You just didn't know it yet," Ariana told me.

"Exactly," Noelle agreed. "So that night, the first night of parents' weekend, we sneaked over to Ketlar to grab him."

"Grab him?" I asked. "How?"

"We knew it wouldn't be a problem, considering how wasted he was, and we were right," Noelle said. "He was so trashed he practically fell into our arms."

She almost laughed then. As if this part of the story was somehow funny. I gripped her silk comforter in my sweaty palms.

"Then what?" I said through my teeth.

"Well, Josh conveniently was not there, but his car keys were," Noelle said. "He'd used it earlier that day and we'd all seen it parked over by the circle."

"So it was close," Ariana said.

"So we took it," Kiran put in.

Suddenly the realization hit me. How Josh's car seats and mirrors had been all out of place on the day of the funeral and he couldn't figure out why. How Taylor hadn't wanted to take Josh's car back to Easton. She'd seemed almost afraid of it. How broken up she'd been that day and every day after that and how I'd never understood why. Constance had theorized that Taylor had been secretly in love with Thomas, but that wasn't it at all. Taylor had killed Thomas. She'd been there when it all happened. Of course she had lost it when the body was found—she was wondering when the police were going to figure out who'd done it.

"We got Thomas in the backseat and we drove out to this farm on the outskirts of Easton. . . ."

Noelle trailed off. The muscles around her mouth twitched. She didn't want to go on.

"What did you do to him?" I said. My voice sounded cold and strange, like it was coming from somewhere outside myself.

"All we wanted to do was humiliate him, Reed," she said. "We just wanted him to feel how you felt that night, so he would understand."

I couldn't believe this was happening. That I was sitting here, in the room I had once so longed to step into, listening to . . . this.

"What did you *do*, Noelle?" I demanded.

"We . . . we . . ."

Noelle's eyes filled with tears.

"We took his shirt off. . . ."

This wasn't real. This was a nightmare. A horror movie. A horror movie about a nightmare that I was never going to wake up from.

"We—"

"Oh, for heaven's sake," Ariana said, stepping into my line of sight. "We took his shirt off and put this black mesh bag over his head. Something one of Kiran's many purses had been wrapped in."

"Versace," Kiran whispered, still half out of it.

"Then we dragged him over to this old scarecrow pole and tied him up there."

Ariana's voice sounded crisp and detached, like she was telling a story about how she'd changed a tire to someone who was too stupid to understand the mechanics of it. Like people tied other people to scarecrow poles every day of the week.

The cruelty of it—the very incomprehensible callousness—brought bile into my mouth. I tried to swallow and glanced at Noelle. She wiped under her eyes and shook her hair back.

"We woke him up," Noelle continued.

"How?" My voice wasn't there, but my mouth formed the word.

"Josh had some bottled water in his car," Ariana said. "We dumped it over his head and shoulders."

A few tears squeezed from my eyes. "So he wakes up with a black bag over his head, tied to a pole," I spat.

"Yes. I know. It sounds bad—"

"It sounds bad, Noelle?" I said, standing. "It *sounds* like you tortured him!"

"Shhhhh!" Noelle put her hands on my shoulders and gently pushed me down again. "We didn't torture him. He was just a little scared, that's all."

"Oh, really?" The tears flowed freely now. "I wonder why."

I thought of Thomas tied up out there in the middle of the night. Drugged. Confused. Unable to defend himself. He must have been *so* scared. So alone. Petrified. These people were evil. I was sitting here letting three evil people describe their crime to me. All the misery, all the confusion, all the bone-crushing sorrow of the past month and a half—it was all thanks to them.

"Reed, we did all of this for you," Ariana said angrily. Angrily. As if she was annoyed by my horror. "We were trying to help you."

"Gee, thanks, Ariana. So when did you start beating him to death?" Her eyes flashed, and for a split second I honestly thought she was going to strangle me. But then, Noelle stepped in front of her.

"Reed, get this through your head. We did not kill Thomas Pearson," she said.

I stared up at her and I wanted to believe her. God help me, I really wanted to believe her.

"Then what did you do?" I managed to say.

"We taunted him," Kiran said, her voice full of exhaustion and tears. "Disguised our voices and asked him how it felt to be exposed. Humiliated. Asked him how he liked it. We wanted to freak him out, so we poked him with some branches and . . . and . . ."

"And Josh's bat," Noelle said.

My stomach heaved and my hand flew to my mouth.

"But that was all we did, Reed. I swear to you," Noelle said. "We did *not* hurt him."

Kiran looked up at us blearily. "He said he wanted to get down. That he couldn't breathe in the hood—"

"But that wasn't true," Ariana said, crossing her arms over her chest. "There were so many tiny holes in that bag he could breathe just fine."

"He was fine when we left him there," Noelle said. "We even loosened the ropes so that he could get free. Once he sobered up some, he should have gotten out of there. He should have been able to find his way back to campus."

"But he never came back," Kiran said.

There was a long moment of silence. I had no idea what to say. What to believe. I just wanted to get out of there. Get away from these people. I just wanted to get away and be able to think.

"There was a while there when Taylor and I thought we might have been responsible," Kiran said. "You know, maybe he really *couldn't* breathe. Maybe—"

"But then they found the bat and determined that it was the murder weapon," Noelle said. "That was when we knew for sure that it had nothing to do with us."

"Somebody must have found him out there after we left," Ariana mused. "Somebody who really didn't like him."

"Or somebody who was just psycho," Kiran added.

"We could never have *killed* him, Reed," Noelle said, her expression disgusted. "You know that, right?"

"Let's say I believe you," I said. "Let's say I believe that you didn't actually kill him. That doesn't change what you just admitted to. How could you do something like that to another person? Drag him out of his home . . . scare him like that . . . *leave* him? What kind of people are you?"

"We're the kind of people who care about you," Ariana replied. "We're the kind of people who would risk everything to do this so that you wouldn't have to be disrespected and spat upon by the guy who was supposedly in love with you."

My head shook. "I never asked you to do this. Don't act like this was somehow a *good* thing. You took him out there. You left him there. Whether or not you swung the bat . . . it doesn't even matter. If you hadn't done what you did, he wouldn't have been out there to get killed. He would still be alive right now!"

Tears spilled over onto my cheeks in waves. I grabbed up my coat and turned to go, but Ariana grabbed the hem and I nearly tripped.

"None of that changes the fact that we only had you in mind," Noelle said, stepping in front of me. "You have no idea what the last few months have been like for us. We did all of this for you, Reed."

"Stop saying that!" I shouted.

"But it's the truth," Noelle continued. "We did it for you. And now you're going to do something for us."

"Oh, am I?" I blurted sarcastically.

"Yes. You are. You are going to keep your mouth shut," Noelle said. "You're not ever going to tell another living soul what you saw, what we just told you."

"No one will believe you even if you try," Ariana added. "Noelle deleted the evidence."

"Don't forget who we are, Reed. What we can do," Noelle reminded me. "If you go to the police or anyone else, you're just going to sound like an insane liar with an active imagination. No one will ever believe that *we* could do something so heinous."

I glared at her, wishing more than anything that she was wrong, but we both knew that she wasn't.

No one would believe me. No one would care.

"I have to go," I said finally.

Noelle smiled kindly, almost pityingly. "Go ahead. Get some rest. We'll talk about this more later."

I took my coat and walked out of the room, knowing that for once, Noelle was wrong. We weren't going to talk about this later. I was never going to speak to any of them again for the rest of my life.

THE RIGHT THING

Natasha was passed out in her bed when I returned to our room. I moved slowly to my bed and sat down, then turned and lay back on the pillows, letting my coat slide to the floor. I could feel this thing looming over me. This huge, thick, dark shadow. It was the truth of Thomas's death. The truth of who these people were. The truth of the people I had worshipped, the people I had followed, the people I had admired more than anyone I'd ever known.

The shadow started to descend. If I let it overtake me, there would be no turning back. I had to do something. I had to keep it from swallowing me whole.

I grabbed my coat off the floor. Every inch of me shook as I dug in my pocket for my cell phone. It wasn't there. I checked the left pocket. Empty. I could have sworn I'd shoved it back in my right pocket earlier. I grabbed my purse. Nothing but a lip gloss and some blotting papers. I checked the floor. The bed. My desk. All the while, my mind was racing and my blood throttled through my veins.

I turned around. Natasha's phone was on her desk. I crossed the room in two steps and grabbed it. I was shaking so hard at this point, I was sure I'd never be able to dial.

Deep breath, Reed. You're doing the right thing.

I opened the phone. No signal.

Of course no signal. Natasha never got a signal in the room. I grabbed up my coat again, shoved my arms into the sleeves. I looked down at my high-heeled sling-backs, which had been slapping against my heels like flip-flops all night. I slipped out of them. My feet were going to freeze, but I didn't intend to be on the roof for long. I opened the door. I thought about not closing it behind me to avoid the noise, but if anyone happened to peek out into the hallway, they'd realize I'd gone. Ever so slowly, I pulled the door closed, then released the knob with a tiny click. I tiptoed down the darkened hallway, past Noelle and Ariana's room, and over to the stairwell. Another door. Another click. And then I was flying up the stairs toward the sky.

Outside, the rooftop was grainy under my feet. And very, very cold. I hugged my coat closer to my body and lifted the phone. That was when I realized I didn't have the number for the local police. Dammit. Should I call 911? Did this qualify as an immediate emergency? I took a chance and checked Natasha's contacts. God bless Miss Responsible. She had the Easton Police Department programmed in.

I hit the send button and held the phone to my ear. As it rang, I could feel my knees shaking. I walked over toward the scalloped wall that lined the roof and looked out across the campus. There was Ketlar, where Thomas once lived and where Josh now slept. There was the quad, where I had first seen Thomas, almost tripped over him, on my first day of school. There was the bench where we'd sat that day he'd fought with Noelle—the day I first realized how deeply I understood him. There was Gwendolyn Hall, where Thomas and I used to meet when we wanted to be alone together in the middle of the day.

On the other end of the phone, a female voice greeted me.

"Easton Police Department, how may I direct your call?"

My grip on the phone tightened. My heart flew to my throat. "Detective Hauer, please."

"One moment, I'll have to track him down."

There was a click and the line started to ring again. Another click. I opened my mouth to speak. To finally let it all out.

And the phone was ripped out of my hand.

MY DEATH

I whirled around. Ariana stood before me, Natasha's phone in her hand. A grim smile contorted her beautiful face.

"What are you doing?" I said, grabbing for the phone.

Ariana shoved me hard with her free hand. I stumbled backward and slammed into the wall as I fell.

"Detective Hauer," a faint voice said. "Hello?"

I tried to suck in air. Tried to cry out for help. Nothing. I'd had the wind knocked out of me before on the playing field. Knew in some recess of my brain that it would come back soon. But it didn't help. I was sick with fear.

"Hello?"

Ariana brought the phone to her ear.

"Oh my God! You have to help me!" she cried, staring coolly into my eyes the entire time. "It's my friend, Reed! She . . . she jumped from the roof of our dorm!" She let out a wail. "I think she's dead! Come! Quickly! Please!"

I could hear Detective Hauer sputtering questions at her as she slowly closed the phone. As the terror clutched my gut, my throat finally opened and my breath came back. I doubled over on the ground, coughing and gasping, even as I was paralyzed with fear.

Ariana placed the phone in her pocket and withdrew a small blade with a pearl handle. She stepped toward me and crouched down, her knees together, ever the lady. The blade was directly beneath my chin. One quick swipe and she could end me.

"Did you really think I was going to let you call the police?" she asked, the venom dripping from her teeth.

She grabbed my coat at the collar and yanked me up off the ground with one quick motion. Her strength astounded me. I tried to throw her arm off, but she just clutched me harder, twisting the collar up under my chin until I could hardly breathe. All the while the knife was there. Right there.

"You did it, didn't you?" I said with a cough. "You killed Thomas."

Ariana's smile widened and she laughed. Slowly she turned me and pushed me backward. I struggled for traction, but my cold feet found only silt.

"No, Reed. *You* killed Thomas," she said. "I have your confession right in my pocket. In your suicide note." A lump the size of a soccer ball lodged in my throat. "It seems poor little Pennsylvania Reed just wasn't cut out for the lifestyle of debauchery here at Easton. According to your note, you snapped once when your perfect new boyfriend cheated on you—just like he did on every other

girl he ever dated. That's what rich boys do, after all. And now
you've snapped again, from the guilt, of course. But this time,
you're just taking your own life."

"No one will believe that," I sputtered.

"Why not? You signed the note," Ariana said placidly. "I'm very
good at forging signatures—did I ever tell you that?"

I twisted awkwardly and looked over my shoulder. She was
taking me to the part of the wall on this side of the building where
the wall had crumbled. It was far lower here than anywhere else on
the roof. All the easier to shove me over.

I was about to die. I was about to *die*.

I grabbed at Ariana's coat sleeve, struggling to pull her off of me.
She flipped the blade around so that the handle was hidden in her
fist, then slammed that fist right across my jaw. My head whipped
sideways and I saw actual stars.

"If you keep fighting me, this is going to get messy," Ariana said
through the ringing in my ears. "Is that what you want?"

Messy. Blood. My blood. Thomas's blood. Ariana had killed
him. She'd taken that bat and she'd killed him. Suddenly my body
went limp. My legs buckled from underneath me and I hit the
ground, weeping.

"You killed him," I wailed, tears streaming down my face.
"Why? Why did you kill him?"

Ariana was crouched down next to me, still holding onto my
coat. She rolled her eyes. "Who knew you were such a drama
queen?"

She tried to yank me up again, but I used my body weight against her and only slid back a few inches. "Tell me! You at least owe me that. You're going to kill me anyway, right? So just tell me!"

"Shut up!"

She struggled to lift me again, managed to slide me back far enough so that my back slammed into the low wall. My head collided with the brick and I winced.

"No. Just tell me why, Ariana!" I shouted. "Why did Thomas have to die? *Why?* Why did you take him away from me?"

Something shifted in Ariana's eyes. I could see all the blood rushing in under her milky white skin.

"Why did *I* take him from *you*!?"

With one, huge burst of adrenaline, she yanked me to my feet again. I had just made one huge mistake.

"I didn't take him from you! You took him from me!" she shouted.

"What are you talking about?" I whispered without meaning to. "You hated him. All the Billings Girls hated him."

"He loved *me*, Reed!" Ariana shouted, as though I hadn't said anything at all. "Me! We were supposed to be together this year! For real! No more sneaking around behind his girlfriends' backs. No more coming in second to all his ridiculous whores! He promised me! He promised me that when we got back to school we would tell everyone. He *promised*! But then *you* had to come along! You came here and you seduced him!"

She nudged me back toward the wall. The fear was paralyzing.

I glanced behind me to see how close I was to my death. My eyes landed on Bradwell. My first dorm here at Easton. The place I'd been so quick to leave in favor of Billings. If only I'd just stayed there, maybe none of this would have happened. Maybe I would have been cozily asleep in my bed in Bradwell right now. But instead I was here on the roof, looking down, about to die.

And then, the rooftop door opened silently behind Ariana. Noelle. For a split second, Noelle's eyes locked with mine. I was just about to scream out for her help when she shook her head. She emerged the rest of the way and I saw that she had a lacrosse stick in her other hand.

"I should have just killed you in the first place," Ariana said through her teeth. "If I had just killed *you*, then Thomas and I would be together now. Together. Like we were supposed to be."

Noelle crept across the rooftop, trying not to make a noise. From the corner of my eye I saw the flashing blue and red lights of the Easton police cars. So far below. So very, very far below.

Ariana backed me up, holding the knife point to my chin. The ground loomed beneath me. My blood rushed through my ears, and all I could hear was the beating of my heart. Just two more seconds. If I could just stall for two more seconds. But what could I do?

"Thomas did love you, Ariana," I blurted. "He told me he did."

Her eyes immediately softened and her jaw dropped. "He did?" Her voice sounded hopeful, and suddenly eerily sweet.

And Noelle slammed the lacrosse stick down across her back.

Ariana fell to her knees and dropped the knife. I grabbed it without even thinking and moved away from the edge of the roof. Moved behind Noelle. My heart was pounding so hard, every beat hurt. But that was because I was alive. I was still alive.

On the floor, Ariana rolled over onto her back. "Noelle," she said. She sounded confused, like she couldn't quite figure out what Noelle was doing up there with us.

"I knew it," Noelle said, narrowing her eyes. "I knew it."

CONFESSION

"You don't know anything," Ariana spat, pushing herself up off the ground.

Noelle reached out and took the knife from my hands, seeming perfectly in control.

"I knew you were up here, didn't I?" Noelle challenged. "I saw you lift Reed's phone from her coat earlier. You knew she'd have to use Natasha's crap phone, and you knew that meant coming up here, where she'd be vulnerable."

Ariana stood there silently. I instinctively took a step back.

"And I also knew you were in love with him," Noelle continued. "Didn't keep that particular secret very well."

A flash of confusion crossed Ariana's face. "H—how?"

"All those pathetic love poems on your computer, Ariana? Please. You saved them under 'TP.' Not the hardest code to break."

I brought my hand to my head. Ariana's computer. Those files with initials for titles. Had there been a TP among them? If I'd just opened that file back then . . . could I have somehow prevented all of this?

"You were always pushing to get Reed into the house," Noelle continued. "Saying we could change the rules for the right girl, setting up Leanne. What was that, Ariana? A keep-your-enemies-closer thing?"

I took a deep breath. It was all so insane. All so completely, totally, beyond insane—but at the same time, it all made such perfect sense.

"Oh, Noelle. You're so very smart," Ariana said, and choked out a laugh. "But you have no proof of anything, so you can drop the high-and-mighty act now. I think we should all go back downstairs and forget that any of this ever happened."

And then *I* almost laughed.

"Come on, Ariana. Indulge an old friend," Noelle said. "Let me tell you what I think happened that night."

"Fine," Ariana said, slowly crossing her arms over her chest. She glanced at me, then returned her gaze to Noelle. "Go ahead." Her attempts to sound calm were no longer working.

"I think that after we came back to school, you lifted Josh's keys from my desk and went back out to the cornfield," Noelle said. "I think you were pissed off at Thomas for being so obviously head over heels for Reed, so you took Josh's bat out of the back of the car and attacked Thomas. You just couldn't stand that he was with yet another girl who wasn't you. So you killed him and then you forged that note to Reed to throw her off your trail."

My stomach clenched. The note. The goodbye note Thomas had left me the night he'd disappeared, in which he'd said he was going somewhere to recover. Thomas hadn't written that note. He had never said goodbye to me. Had never had the chance. "You're already wrong," Ariana said with a smile. A smile. I could have killed her right then myself.

"Please. We all know that's what happened," Noelle said.

Ariana just stared at her with those icy blue eyes. I felt a chill rush right through me. Noelle dropped her lacrosse stick on the floor and stepped forward with the knife. She held the point right beneath Ariana's nose.

"I have spent this entire semester covering your ass, Ariana," she said. "It's over now. I think I deserve to know the truth."

Ariana smirked. "Or what, you're gonna kill me?"

In one swift motion, Noelle pressed the knife blade to Ariana's throat. Ariana gasped.

"No!" I shouted automatically.

I could see the indentation of the blade in Ariana's skin. For the first time since I'd known her, there was fear in Ariana's eyes.

"Now we know what *you're* capable of," Noelle said quietly. "Do you really want to find out what *I'm* capable of?"

One fat tear rolled out of Ariana's eye and down her cheek. "Okay," she said. And then she breathed a heavy sigh. "I'll tell you."

Noelle stepped back and Ariana covered her face with her gloved hands. Her tiny shoulders shook as she sobbed, her cries muffled by her gloves. Somewhere on campus a door slammed.

"It wasn't like that!" Ariana cried, letting her hands drop. "I didn't just attack him! I went back to untie him. To let him go. I loved him, Noelle. I *loved* him. I couldn't just *leave* him there in the cold all scared and alone. I loved him!"

"Oh, really? Then how the hell did he end up with his head bashed in?" Noelle demanded.

"He *made* me do it!" Ariana wailed. "When I took his hood off, he freaked out, screaming and yelling. He spat in my face. He was calling me a whore. Saying I would never be good enough for him. He was saying he was going to turn us in. I couldn't have that! I couldn't let him do that to us!"

She was sobbing as she shouted. Her face was blotched and red and soaked with tears. She held her stomach and bent at the waist as she gasped for breath.

"So you killed him," Noelle said flatly.

"No! I . . . the . . . the bat was still on the ground, and I was just going to threaten him with it. That was all! I never meant to hurt him. But he just kept screaming at me and calling me these filthy things and I . . . I had to make him stop! I had to make him stop!"

Ariana doubled over, incoherent. She braced one hand against the ground for a moment, but then she just collapsed. She just collapsed at our feet and cried. Behind us, the door opened. Detective Hauer emerged with his gun drawn, followed by three men in uniform. His eyes were relieved when he saw me.

"It's your fault, Reed," Ariana choked out, sputtering at the floor. "I killed Thomas, but you made me! Why did you have to come here? You ruined everything!"

That was all Detective Hauer needed to hear. He brushed past me and Noelle and grabbed Ariana around the forearm, hauling her to her feet.

"Ariana Osgood, you are under arrest for the murder of Thomas Pearson," he said, as one of the officers came forward to handcuff her. "You have the right to remain silent. Anything you say can and will be used against you in a court of law. . . ."

Ariana continued to weep as they walked her past us. She tipped her face forward and her blond hair fell over her cheeks, hiding her from sight. Ariana was the first of the Billings Girls to really talk to me. She had been my first friend here. The skin on my face prickled and the rest of me felt numb. Two hours ago we were all laughing and chatting in the limousine, warm and cocooned together. Friends.

"What just happened?" I said to Noelle, tears spilling down my cheeks. "What just happened?"

She stepped forward and put her arms around me. I crumpled into her, my whole body shaking with sobs.

"It's okay, Reed," she said quietly. "Everything's going to be okay now."

"Miss? Could I have the knife, please?"

One of the officers held his hand out to Noelle. We both looked up. I hadn't even realized she was still holding it. She turned it so that the handle was forward and handed it to him. He nodded his thanks.

"Anyone want to try explaining what happened up here?" he asked.

I dried my eyes with my hands. Noelle and I looked at one another. Who knew where or how to start? Then Detective Hauer returned and dismissed the other officers. They scurried off obediently.

"Good to see you alive," he told me.

"Thanks," I said.

"Are you all right, Ms. Lange?" he asked Noelle.

She nodded. "You're going to want to arrest me, too, Detective," she said. Her voice had this odd detachment I had never heard before. Like she was talking to us from some other plane. "I have a confession to make as well."

His eyebrows shot up.

"Noelle—"

"No, Reed. It's enough. I've had enough. It's time to end this," she said. She looked at Detective Hauer and her playful smile lit her eyes for a brief moment. "Got any more handcuffs?"

He eyed her warily but then placed his hand on her back. "I don't think that will be necessary just yet," he said. "Why don't we all go back to the station and you two can tell me the whole story? Then we can decide who gets cuffs and who doesn't."

Noelle took a deep breath and shook her hair back. Always poised. "Sounds fair to me."

She walked ahead of us, and Detective Hauer touched my arm lightly, holding me back. "You gonna help me sort all this out?" he asked.

I looked around the roof, at the spot where Ariana had knocked the wind out of me, the crumbling wall where I'd almost met my death, the lacrosse stick that had saved me, still lying on the floor. The hands that had killed Thomas had almost killed me tonight.

The hands that had killed Thomas.

I looked into the detective's eyes and whispered, "I'll try."

NEW RULES

I was exempt from finals. When everything was taken into account—one boyfriend dead, another falsely accused, and an attempt on my life by a supposed friend—it all resulted in me finally being deemed a charity case. So on that Monday morning, when the rest of my history class was scratching away in their blue books, I was packing my bags.

The room looked bare without my stuff. My sheets shoved into my laundry bag, my books stuffed into my backpack. By leaving everything the Billings Girls had ever given me in the closet, I was able to fit all my clothes back in the one suitcase I'd brought with me in September. I wanted to start over. And if that meant going back to being the old me—cotton instead of cashmere, nylon instead of silk—I was fine with that.

I picked up my cell phone and stared at the blank screen. I'd taken it back from Noelle and Ariana's room the day before, but I'd yet to turn it on. There would be messages on there, I knew. From my brother, whom I'd e-mailed. From my dad, whom I'd asked my brother to talk to. From Josh? Maybe. Hopefully. But part of the reason I hadn't turned it on was that I didn't want to find out if he hadn't called.

My digital watch beeped, startling me. The history exam was over, which meant it was time to meet Constance for lunch. I pushed myself off my bare bed, pocketed the phone, and paused at the door. Would I ever see this room again? I had no idea. There was a decision to be made about my future, but I didn't feel remotely ready to make it yet. As I looked around the room, though, I felt nothing at the thought of leaving it behind forever. Not that I was surprised. Since wrapping up my interview with the police on Sunday morning, I'd been numb. I'd barely felt anything at all.

I closed the door behind me. Down the hall, the door to Kiran and Taylor's room was open. I wandered over to it. Leaned in the doorway. The place was completely empty, save for the Easton-issue furniture. The maintenance staff had come in that morning and packed up everything from the two bedrooms. The blinds had been thrown open to let the winter sun in. All of Kiran's coats and shoes and makeup were gone, all of Ariana's books and scarves and sweaters, all of Noelle's tons and tons of crap. Just days ago, they were here. Hanging out. Studying. Trying to pretend everything was normal.

My heart constricted and I took a sharp breath of surprise. I was going to miss them. Even after everything. I was going to miss them. Or the people I had thought they were. The people who had promised to give me everything. The people who were supposed to change my life.

"Hey."

I turned around to find Natasha hovering behind me. She wore her lucky sweater—a blue cardigan with leather patches on the sleeves that belonged to her dad.

"Hey. How was your test?" I asked.

"Piece of cake," she said with a small, wry smile. "I just stopped by our room. It's kind of empty."

I said nothing. Looked back at the barren room before us.

"You don't have to take everything, you know. They do lock up the dorms."

"I know," I said.

There was a long moment of silence. I braced myself for the questions. The ones I couldn't answer.

"So, did you hear they arrested Taylor?" she asked.

Not at all what I expected her to say. I whipped around. "They did? When? Where was she?"

"Back home in Chicago," Natasha said. "She's been in public school for the past three weeks, if you can believe it."

"You're kidding." So not at a treatment facility, as Noelle and the others had told me. Not having a psychotic break. *Whatever they told you about me is not true*, she'd written in her e-mail. The words finally made sense.

"Apparently her parents thought Easton was a bad influence on her, so they changed her e-mail and phone numbers and enrolled her out there," Natasha said.

"A bad influence, huh?" I said. "Where would they get that idea?"

Natasha exhaled and smiled.

"What's going to happen to her?" I wondered. "To all of them?"

Natasha leaned back against the wall in the hallway. "They'll charge Ariana with murder, or maybe manslaughter if her lawyer kicks ass and declares temporary insanity. The rest of them . . . at the very least, they'll be charged with kidnapping, assault, endangerment," she said. "But if they really want to make an example of them, they charge them with aiding and abetting, both before and after the fact."

"Wow. How do you know all this?" I asked.

"I'm going to be a lawyer," she said matter-of-factly. "Anyway, you can bet they're going to have the best criminal attorneys in the country. Noelle, Kiran, and Taylor? They may just get off with a slap."

A rush of heat lit my face. "No."

"Yeah," Natasha said. Then she added, apologetically, "It's the world we live in."

My throat had all but closed up. I had no idea how to feel about that revelation. I wanted them to be punished for what they'd done to Thomas, but then Noelle, Kiran, and Taylor . . . they were still my friends. My friends who had made a huge, stupid mistake, but my friends. If they didn't have to rot in prison, that would be a good thing.

Except that they should. They should be punished. For what they did to him. For how scared he must have been . . .

I shoved the thoughts away. Couldn't deal with them now. Couldn't deal with them ever.

"I get Noelle's side!"

"Fine by me. I like the window."

Cheyenne and Rose emerged from the stairwell toting boxes and hangers full of clothes. They shoved open the door to Noelle and Ariana's room and bustled inside.

"What the . . . ?"

Natasha and I moved across the hall to the doorway. Rose was already hanging her things in Ariana's closet, while Cheyenne inspected the dust on Noelle's desk. She ran her finger across it and wrinkled her nose.

"What are you doing?" I asked.

"Lattimer said we could move in," Cheyenne said casually, slapping her fingers to clean them. "It *is* the best room in the house, and it's not like they're coming back."

I swallowed a lump in my throat.

"You couldn't at least wait until next semester?" Natasha asked.

Cheyenne shrugged as she opened the box on the bed. "Someone was going to take it. We just wanted to make sure we got here first."

"God, Cheyenne. Could you be any more callous?" Natasha asked.

Cheyenne was amused. "Natasha, you're acting like Noelle and

Ariana did nothing wrong. They murdered someone, for goodness'
sake." She glanced at my rapidly paling face. "No offense."

"None taken," I croaked.

"The point is, they got themselves kicked out. Let's not martyr
them, okay?" Cheyenne said.

She pulled her satin jewelry box out of the cardboard one and
placed it atop Noelle's dresser. The dresser behind which I'd once
found that envelope full of naked pictures of Dash—the ones Noelle
had planted for me to find as a joke. I smiled at the memory now,
even as my eyes filled with tears. This was ridiculous. Twenty-four
hours of numb and now, all of a sudden, I was feeling everything all
at once.

"I have to go," I said.

"That's right! I heard you were leaving early," Cheyenne said.
She stepped up to me and gave me a quick hug, pressing her face
into my shoulder. "Have a fantastic break, Reed. Just try to put this
semester behind you, because next semester everything is going to
be different."

I attempted to smile. Different. Right. How could it not be?

"I can't wait!" Cheyenne trilled.

At that moment Vienna and London burst in, Vienna in her pink
coat, London in her baby blue, both with white wool hats pulled
down over their thick hair.

"Cheyenne Martin! What do you think you're doing?" London
demanded.

"I'm moving into my new room," Cheyenne said.

"Oh, no way!" Vienna said, tossing her sweater bag on Noelle's bed. "This is *our* room. Our mothers were both in Billings, which means we have pri!"

"You can*not* just take the good room," London said. "That is just nonacceptable."

"I think you mean *un*acceptable," Natasha corrected.

"Whatever. My brain is mush from that history final," London said. "The point is, we're moving in here. Not you. We'll stage a sit-down if we have to."

"That would be a sit-*in*, sweetie," Vienna said, whipping her hat off. "And that's exactly what we'll do."

"Girls, girls, girls," Cheyenne said, shaking her head. "Do you really think it's appropriate to cause a scene right now considering all that's happened?"

Vienna and London looked at one another as if they were suddenly embarrassed.

"Oh . . . well . . . yeah. Of course. What happened with Noelle and them is awful," Vienna said.

"Just terrible," London agreed.

There was a moment of silence. Rose continued organizing her clothes.

"But still! That doesn't mean you can just swoop in here and change the rules!" Vienna protested.

Natasha laughed under her breath.

"Might I suggest a compromise?" Cheyenne said. She hooked her arm around London's back, then reached out for Vienna as well.

Sandwiched between their big-haired curviness, Cheyenne looked even tinier and wirier than ever. "You two can have Kiran and Taylor's room! The view from there is just as pretty."

"Yeah, but—"

"And you know, I was thinking that next semester we could implement an interior governing system for Billings. You know, like a real sorority," Cheyenne continued. "How would you two girls feel about being co—social chairs?"

The Twin Cities stared at each other, wide-eyed.

"What, exactly, would our powers be?" London asked.

"Well, we'd need to figure that out as we went along of course, but I'm thinking event planning, decorating, invitations. . . ."

London and Vienna were nodding in unison. Cheyenne really knew how to play to her audience. Natasha rolled her eyes at me and together we walked out. In the hallway I was surprised to find that I was smiling. The Twin Cities were always good for that.

"Well. Sounds like next semester is gonna be a blast," Natasha said with false enthusiasm. "I can't wait to get back. How about you?" she asked pointedly.

"Yeah," I said, my smile faltering. "Can't wait."

RETURN TO BRADWELL

"I'm thinking about not coming back."

Constance tripped over the leg of her chair and then fell into it, dropping her tray on the table with a clatter. Her face was a picture of devastation. She was wearing those braids again, the ones that made her look ten years old. I felt like I'd just kicked Little Orphan Annie in the gut.

"What? No," she said.

I shrugged and looked down at my untouched sandwich. The door opened and I tried my hardest not to look up at the people entering. I had no idea how I'd act if I saw Josh. I felt so incredibly, monumentally stupid and guilty and chagrined and sad every time I thought about him. Part of me felt that if I saw him I would just burst into tears, which would not help the feeling-stupid part. But part of me was aching to see him so badly I could have keeled over from the pain.

"Reed, everything is going to be different now," Constance said, shaking her bottle of Snapple. "They're gone. We all know who killed Thomas. It's over. Next semester everything's going to go back to normal."

"Yeah, but what is that?" I asked, desperation twisting in my chest. "Since I've been here, it's been all about Noelle and then Thomas and then Josh. . . . I don't even know what normal *is* here."

"So don't you want to find out?" Constance asked. Her eyes sparkled with excitement. I wished I could feel that. I really did. But all I felt was overwhelmed. And tired. And thoroughly confused.

"I don't know. It's not like I'm dying to go back to Croton High," I said. Just imagining the gray cinderblock walls, the institutional lockers, the dingy cafeteria with its fading READING IS FUNDAMENTAL posters made me sad. "But it might be a better alternative to starting over again at Billings."

Constance eyed me sympathetically. Then, right before my eyes, her entire face lit up. A total transformation. "So don't go back to Billings!"

"What?"

"Yes! You can come back and live with me!" she suggested, grabbing my hand and shaking it on the table. "Omigod! It'll be so much fun! Like it should have been!"

Damn, she was sweet. She was so sweet she was spewing gumdrops.

"I don't know. . . ."

"Come on! I'm sick of my single anyway," she said, raising her eyebrows. "Let's be roommates again."

I took a deep breath and considered. Considered how simple that would be. Maybe if I did go back, I could just fly under the radar. Do my work. Be a student. Maybe there would be no more fabulous balls and flowing champagne. No more expensive gifts and spa treatments. Maybe when I graduated, I wouldn't have the support of the Billings Girls and all their connections behind me. But at least there would be no drama.

No drama. I liked the sound of that.

"Maybe," I said finally, not wanting to get her hopes up too high.

"Yes! This is going to be so totally beyond amazing!"

Constance jumped out of her seat and hugged me across the table. I rolled my eyes but smiled. I'd forgotten who I was talking to. With Constance, she'd get her hopes up as high as she wanted, thank you very much.

CLOSED

It was a beautiful day. Warm for December. I didn't even need a hat as I stood on the circle in front of Bradwell, waiting for my father to arrive. The campus was silent, everyone sequestered in their class-rooms, taking their exams. All of them together, struggling through, heading for the finish line and their fabulous vacations. Me out here alone, waiting for the station wagon, the long ride home.

I turned and looked up at the buildings around the circle. They seemed smaller than before. Maybe because I knew what went on inside those walls now. Knew it wasn't all honor and truth and excellence. It was sad, really, how much my view of this place had changed. I remembered that first day when we had pulled up here. Remembered how sophisticated and intelligent everyone had looked. How privileged I'd felt just to be here. I remembered meet-ing Constance and how I'd thought we could never be friends—that her incessant talking would drive me insane. How wrong I had been about her. I remembered Thomas, his knowing eyes, his self-assuredness, his sexy smile. And seeing the girls through the window at Bradwell. Noelle. Ariana. Kiran. Taylor. How exotic they had seemed then.

A tear slipped down my cheek and I quickly wiped it away.

I heard the chug of my father's car as it turned up the hill down below. And suddenly I couldn't wait to get out of here.

I picked up my backpack and shouldered it. That was when I heard the footsteps pounding behind me. I turned around and Josh grabbed me up in his arms.

"I caught you. Thank God," he said, squeezing me hard. Squeezing out a few extra tears. I was relieved and anguished all at once. Wanted him to keep on holding me forever and also to just let me go.

"Josh, I . . . your test—"

"Who cares? Are you okay? I heard you were leaving and I—are you okay?" He was grasping me all over. My shoulders, then my elbows, then my hips. Like he was checking to see if any parts of me were broken. His hands landed, finally, on my cheeks, cupping my face. His face was ruddy from the run, his blue eyes bright. His curly blond hair danced in the breeze. "Are you okay?" he repeated.

"I'm fine," I told him, my heart bursting. "I'm totally fine."

"I've been trying to call you over and over and over, but—"

"My phone was off," I said.

"Why?"

"I don't know." I didn't anymore. That decision made zero sense to me now. "I just thought if you didn't call then I'd . . . I'm sorry. It's just been—"

"I know. I'm sorry." He held me close and then let me go and looked at me again. "You don't have to talk about it if you don't want to," he said.

I exhaled. "Thanks. I can't. Not . . . yet."

"I'm glad I got here in time," he said. "I had to say goodbye to you."

I held his hand and listened to the approach of my father's car. I couldn't speak. Had no idea what to say.

"Reed, I'm so sorry for what happened at the party. I was still kind of raw, you know? From everything that had happened. But I know I can't tell you what to do . . . who to hang out with." He squeezed my hand. "I just . . . didn't want you to leave without telling you that."

The Subaru finally appeared at the top of the hill. My heart felt sick at the sight of it now. There was no time left. And so much to say.

"But maybe I can make it all up to you next semester," Josh said. I looked up at him. Looked him dead in the eye. After all that had happened, after all that had been revealed, there was no hint of I-told-you-so, not the tiniest glimmer of I-was-right in Josh's eyes. There was just concern and caring and something else even deeper than that.

My heart pounded erratically. "But Josh . . . I'm not coming back."

All the color seeped right out of him. "What?"

The Subaru turned onto the circle. No time. No time.

"I can't come back here. I can't. It's all wrong," I railed, desperation welling inside of me. "It's just too much. I can't . . . I can't. . . ."

Josh grabbed me and hugged me. "Don't say that," he said into my ear. "Do not say that. You don't have to decide anything right now. Go home. Think about it over break. Just don't—"

I pulled away from him. It was the hardest thing I'd ever done in my life. "I've already made my decision. I'm sorry."

"But Reed, I lo—"

"Don't!" I blurted. My heart was in my throat. The last guy who'd said that to me had gotten killed for it. "Just don't."

Josh stared at me. The hurt and betrayal in his eyes were almost more than I could take. My father stopped the car with a squeal of the brakes. God love him, he didn't get right out.

"This is goodbye," I said.

Then I leaned in and kissed him firmly on the lips. Tears leaked out the corners of my eyes as my heart broke down the middle. I turned around and grabbed my laundry bag. My father took that as his cue. He got out, came around the car, and hugged me. The smell of my dad, the feel of him, almost sent me over the edge. The last time I'd seen my dad was the day he'd dropped me off when every single thing had been different. The sob was right there at the back of my mouth, but I held it.

"Hey, kiddo," my father said, touching my face with his glove.

"You okay?" He looked over at Josh, as if wondering if he'd have to kick some ass.

"M'fine," I replied. "Let's just go."

Without another word, he threw all my stuff in the car and slammed the door. I looked out the window at Josh. He hadn't moved an inch. He just stood there, staring at me, his eyes swimming, his jaw clenched. I touched the window with my fingertips. Still, he didn't move.

The car lurched forward and then pulled away. I looked back once and instantly regretted it. Josh stood there, alone, with those imposing buildings rising up behind him. He loved me. And I was never going to see him again. This was the last image I would have of him, burned into my brain.

I turned around and faced forward. As the car dipped down the hill, I fought the urge to look back again, to see Easton for one last time. I didn't need to see it. It didn't matter. It was over. This chapter of my life was closed.

MY LIFE

Christmas Day. I sat on the curb in front of Wendy's, watching my brother and his friends pop lame-ass tricks on their skateboards in the parking lot. Jen O'Connell and Melissa Pilotowski smoked cigarettes and attempted to peel the numbers off the drive-through menu with a plastic knife they'd found in the bushes. Overhead, the sky was gray, but there was no snow on the ground, no snow in the forecast. Nothing to soften the square blandness of this crusty town. I took a deep breath and looked toward the town center, at the decorations I'd so looked forward to seeing. Their lights were extinguished now, being that it was daylight. The cheap, plastic-covered wires, the tinsel . . . it all just looked depressing now.

A white, mud-splashed Croton police car turned into the parking lot. One whoop of the siren. The window rolled down. It was John Foley. He'd graduated from Croton High two years ago, second to last in his class. Now he was one of Croton's finest.

"All right, kids. Let's move it along," he said.

"You got it, Johnny Fo!" my brother said, lining up for another rail slide.

"I mean now, Brennan," John said. "Not *after* you break your neck."

"Oh, you mean *now*. Like *now* now?" Scott said, earning some laughter from his boys. "Sorry. I misunderstood."

Then he did the slide anyway, dropped down in front of me, and laughed. "Come on, loser. Let's go wake up Mom and force-feed her some Yuletide ham steak."

Yes. This was my life.

I let Scott yank me to my feet by my wrist, then waved goodbye to the others before we headed for home. Adam Robinson, my ex-boyfriend, and Larry Shale fell into step with us. They lived on the next block.

"So, what're you guys doing tomorrow?" Adam asked. "Wanna go to the mall?"

Right. The mall on the day after Christmas to fight all the bargain shoppers. So what I wanted to do.

"Reed?" he asked hopefully.

I was saved from answering by the trill of my cell phone. The one thing Noelle had given me that I had not trashed or stashed. The caller I.D. read RESTRICTED NUMBER. Color me intrigued.

"Sorry. I have to take this," I said.

"Oh, yeah. She's very important now," Scott joked.

I stopped and waited for them to get ahead of me, then answered the phone.

"Hello?"

"Hey, Glass-licker."

My heart thumped extra hard.

"Noelle."

"Got it in one. I always knew you were smart."

My mouth hung open. John Foley rolled by ever so slowly in his black-and-white car, eyeing me like he thought I might suddenly start shooting up the Wal-Mart. I started walking again and he zoomed off.

"What's . . . what's up?" I asked, because I couldn't choose just one of the thousands of questions crowding my mind.

"What's up is I hear you're not going back to Easton," she said.

My grip on the phone tightened so hard I thought it might shatter. "How did you hear that where you are? Where *are* you, by the way?"

"They decided I was a flight risk, so I'm in what they call a juvenile rehabilitation center until my lawyer can figure out some kind of plea," Noelle said, sounding bored by it all. "They don't even have TiVo here."

I laughed. Couldn't help it. This was all too bizarre.

"But enough about my lovely vacay. What are you thinking? Are you going to stay in Crass-ton and become a fry cook or something?"

I stared at my feet as I walked. "There's no point in going back to Easton."

"No point? No point in getting a world-class education that

millions of kids across the country would kill for?" she asked. There was a pause. "Dear God, I think I'm turning into my mother."

"It just doesn't feel right there," I said.

"Oh, and it feels right there? Hanging out with the same lame-ass people in some parking lot somewhere?"

Dear God. She really *did* know everything.

"Reed, Easton is not the place you think it is," Noelle said. "It's not the place we made it for you."

The serious tone of her voice brought a lump to my throat. I tried hard to swallow it down.

"You can still have all the things you went there for. An Ivy League education. A scholarship. A real life."

I looked around at the Stop and Shop with the bird's nest built into the curve of the first *S*, the droppings splattered all over. I looked at the beat-up Ford in the parking lot with the orange FOR SALE sign in the window. I looked toward downtown and beyond, where Croton High sat like a giant, rotting gray mushroom atop a hill of brown grass.

"You're better than that place you came from, Reed," Noelle said quietly in my ear. "Trust me on this. I know better when I see it."

There was a warmth growing inside my chest that surprised me. Up ahead, my brother and his friends turned the corner. They didn't look back.

"Noelle, I appreciate what you're saying. I do. But—"

"Don't let our mistakes screw up your life," Noelle said.

I took a deep breath and blew it out.

"And besides, if you don't go back there, that plastic robot Cheyenne is going to take over, and if that happens, Billings is going right downhill."

I laughed.

"Promise me you'll go back, Reed," Noelle said, her voice full. "I kept saying I was going to protect you, and I did a pretty heinous job of it. This is me trying to make up for that. Go back to Easton. You can have the life you've always wanted."

I held my breath. Closed my eyes. Saw Billings House as it was the first time I walked through the doors. Saw Natasha and Rose and London and Vienna and Cheyenne. Saw Easton. Saw Constance. Saw Dash. Saw Josh.

Josh.

The warmth inside of me grew. When I saw these things, I saw home. When I opened my eyes, I saw Croton.

I knew where I wanted to be.

"Okay, Noelle," I said, smiling. "I'll go back."

"Promise," she said.

"I promise."

A new year.

A new start.

A new inner circle.

Does Reed have what it takes to take charge of the Billings Girls? You'll find out in the fifth book of the Private series,

INNER CIRCLE

And . . . one lucky winner will pose as a Billings Girl on the cover of *Inner Circle*.

In bookstores August 2007

A whole new year
awaits you at Easton Academy.

He's perfect.

If only he were real.

by Kate Brian

In stores December 2007